Jeremy Q Taylor

&

The Cyborg In The Cellar

S. PEPPER

BALBOA.
PRESS

A DIVISION OF HAY HOUSE

Balboa Press books may be ordered through booksellers or by contacting:
Balboa Press
A Division of Hay House
1663 Liberty Drive
Bloomington, IN 47403
www.balboapress.com
1-(877) 407-4847

Printed in the United States of America.

ISBN: 978-1-4525-8103-3 (sc)
ISBN: 978-1-4525-8105-7 (hc)
ISBN: 978-1-4525-8104-0 (e)

Library of Congress Control Number: 2013915452

Balboa Press rev. date: 09/24/2013

*For Dave and Lauren
and sci-fi loving souls everywhere.*

CONTENTS

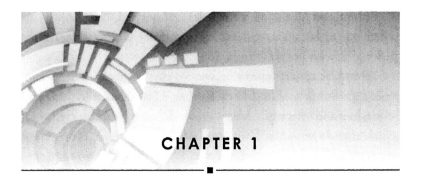

CHAPTER 1

■

ADDISON WHO?

hat in the heck is Dad up to? sixteen-year-old Jeremy
Taylor thought to himself as he stuffed his e-tablet into
his backpack after the final bell. As he and his classmates
made their way to the front doors of the school, he began to feel a sense
of excitement. "Freedom!" he exclaimed as he ran through the doors
into the bright sunlight. "Until tomorrow," he added under his breath
as he motioned to his best friend, Al Duffy, to join him.

The boys made their way through Gilroy High School's parking lot
to Jeremy's fiery-red Mustang convertible. His dad had bought him the
car the year before, after his mother had died. Jeremy's dad, Bob, had
wanted to cheer him up a little—Jeremy missed his mom very much.
They had been so close.

It was late in the afternoon on a beautiful spring day in Silicon
Valley, California, but Jeremy was pensive. "You and Alex have to come
over after dinner," Jeremy said to Al while unlocking the car doors.
"Dad's unveiling his big surprise tonight. Remember how I told you
how he's been working on something downstairs in the basement for
a really long time? It's been, like, a whole year, and I just don't know
what to expect! He says it's a big deal and that I'll love it. But what if I
don't?" Jeremy got into the driver's seat while Al eagerly jumped into
the passenger's seat.

1

"Hmm, no idea at all what it is?" Al queried. "Hey, Alex!" Al yelled, spying his sister working her way down the steps toward the parking lot with her girlfriends.

Al and Alexandra were twins but couldn't be more different. They looked absolutely nothing like each other; Al was short and thin, with brown hair and eyes, while Alex was blonde haired and blue eyed, with a little roundness to her. The twins had differing opinions on almost any topic and had varying likes and dislikes. Al loved sports and cars, while Alex excelled in math and science.

Alex waved, said good-bye to her friends, and ran to the car. She hopped into the backseat. "Let's go!" she exclaimed with a wave of her hand.

Jeremy started the car, listened to it rumble sweetly as he put it in gear, and headed for the school exit. "Alex, can you and Al come over after dinner?" Jeremy asked.

"Don't see why not. What's up?"

"It's his dad," Al chimed in. "He has some sort of surprise for Jeremy that he's been working on for a year."

"Oh, yeah. I kinda remember you mentioning that a while back. You still don't have *any* idea what it is?" Alex asked, perplexed. "You never tried to find out?"

"I went down in the basement once to see what he was doing," Jeremy replied, "but he told me not to go down there. He said he was making me something very special and that I'd find out soon enough! He made me promise not to snoop until he was done. So now he's finished it—whatever *it* is—and I'm kinda nervous. I'm afraid I might not like it . . . you know, Dad's kinda weird sometimes, and ever since Mom died, he's been acting even weirder. Remember when he invented the inflatable swimsuit? What a bad idea that was!" Jeremy burst out laughing.

"Yeah, that was a trip! Remember, Alex, when we went to the Santa Cruz beach and watched Jeremy try out the new swimsuit in the water? He floated on top like a buoy!" Al was laughing as he poked fun at Jeremy. "You looked ridiculous!"

"You couldn't touch the bottom, remember, Jeremy? It was a good thing we were there and Al rescued you, or you'd be in Hawaii by now!"

"How could I forget! That's exactly what I'm talking about. What if Dad invented something like that again? I need you there tonight, in case I need help again!"

"No worries," Alex replied, brushing aside her long, blonde hair from her face. "We'll be there. Hey, can you put the top up, Jeremy? I'm a little cold."

Jeremy looked in his rearview mirror for a moment, at Alex. "Sure, no problem," Jeremy responded. *She's awesome,* he thought to himself. He'd liked her ever since he first laid eyes on her in preschool.

Jeremy pulled up to Al's and Alex's home, and they jumped out of the car. "See you around seven?" Jeremy asked.

"See you then. Bye!" Al waved as he headed to the front door.

Alex got to the door first, opened it, and then turned to wave at Jeremy. "See you later!"

Jeremy waved back and put the car in gear. He rounded the corner of the road and headed into his garage. *Whew,* he thought. *It'll be great to have some friends over tonight. There's safety in numbers!* He parked the car and went inside.

Inside, his aunt Essie was busily working on dinner. "Hi, Jeremy!" she said, glancing up from the stove. "We're having tofu and broccoli for dinner. It's a new recipe, and I think it'll be fabulous!" Essie smiled widely as she cut the tofu into one-inch cubes.

"Yeah, sounds great," Jeremy replied weakly as he sat down at the kitchen table to watch Essie put all the ingredients for the dish into the glass pan.

A cheery jingle of dog tags and the scrabbling of nails on hardwood alerted Jeremy to another presence. His face lit up as the terrier mix slid into the kitchen. He reached out to rub the floppy ears playfully. "Hey there, Sammy boy," Jeremy said softly as the dog sniffed at his hands, no doubt looking for a goodie or treat of some sort. "Has Aunt Essie been starving you again?"

3

Aunt Essie shot Jeremy a look as she threw the tofu into the casserole with more force than was necessary. "I'll have you know that Sammy enjoys his vegetarian diet," she sniffed.

Essie was Jeremy's father's sister. She had come to live with them after Jeremy's mother had died the year before. He loved his aunt dearly, but her cooking was something else. She was a staunch vegetarian, and her cooking style wasn't something Jeremy liked very much, but he appreciated her efforts in the kitchen. It beat the half-frozen TV dinners and stale cola he and his father had been living on prior to her joining their household. Essie was also into yoga and taught a women's class in their living room several times a week. Both Jeremy and his dad were glad that she had moved in with them. It was nice to have a female presence in the house again.

"Your dad's downstairs working. He said for you to stay up here, and he'll be up in a while for dinner."

"I invited Al and Alex over after dinner for the big surprise," Jeremy informed her. He played with Sammy's ears some more, while the dog stared up at him balefully. "They'll be over around seven. I hope that's okay with you."

"Of course, Jeremy. They're welcome anytime. And I don't know about you, but I can't wait to see what Bob invented this time!" Essie replied as she put the broccoli into the baking pan and turned on the oven. "He was a lot of fun to grow up with, making all those strange inventions of his," she added, sliding the pan into the oven and closing the door. "You just never knew what your dad was going to come up with!"

A while later, Aunt Essie and Jeremy heard footsteps coming up the basement stairs. Bob opened the door and, seeing Jeremy, grabbed him into a bear hug. "Hey, son," he said. "Are you ready to see what I've been doing down in the cellar all these months?"

"Yeah, Dad. By the way, I invited Al and Alex to come over and see it too; they'll be here right after dinner," Jeremy told him. "They want to see what you made too. Is that okay?"

"Sure is," Bob replied. "It'll be fun to have your friends here for this. Especially Alex. She gets into the science and seems to enjoy my inventions a lot."

Bob worked at a company in Silicon Valley that made robotics for homes and businesses. After his wife had died, Bob had brought home the latest—and, Jeremy thought, the coolest—robot ever created, the Botman 5000, to help with the chores around the house. The Botman not only walked but could also turn himself into a motorcycle with the touch of a switch on his side. He stood about five feet tall and had very humanlike features but a metallic-silvery color to him. His eyes were an intense sky blue, backlit by LEDs. The Botman walked somewhat haltingly into the kitchen, greeting everyone.

"Hello, Mr. Taylor, Jeremy, Ms. Essie. Can I get you something to drink?" The robot's voice was monotone, with no real inflections.

"No, thank you, Botty," Aunt Essie replied. "I've already taken care of drinks for dinner. But you can take out the trash for me."

"Yes, Ms. Essie," Botty replied, grabbing the trash can jerkily. He lifted the pail in the kitchen and walked slowly to the door that led to the garage, opened it, and pulled the can out with him, letting the door close behind him.

"I love that robot, Bob," Aunt Essie said, smiling, as she watched Botty go. "I have to say, he is such a help to me around here."

"I'm glad to hear you say that, Essie," Bob responded happily. "You know Rob and I worked hard on the prototype."

"You guys work great together, don't you?" Essie asked while taking their dinner out of the oven.

"Yeah," Bob replied. "Hey, dinner looks wonderful. I'm starved!"

"I know you like tofu and broccoli. I made it for this very special occasion."

"Thanks, sis!"

"You're welcome. Let's eat. Botty?"

"Yes, Ms. Essie?" Botty entered the room with the newly emptied wastebasket in hand.

"We're ready for dinner. Can you serve us?"

"Of course, Ms. Essie." He put away the wastebasket and came over to spoon the casserole onto everyone's plates.

"Thanks, Botty," Aunt Essie said, taking a bite. "Mmmm, is that good! What do you boys think?"

Both Bob and Jeremy took bites of the food and nodded in the affirmative. Jeremy, sensing that Sammy was underneath the table by his feet, took a big piece of the casserole off his plate when his aunt wasn't looking and dropped it to the floor. The dog immediately gobbled it up. *Good thing he's a lot less picky than I am about what he eats*, thought Jeremy to himself.

A little while later, there was a knock on the door. Jeremy answered it and invited his friends in. Essie waved a hello and then motioned for them to sit down.

"Hi, kids," she said, pointing to some chairs in the living room. "Have a seat. Would you two like some tofu and broccoli? We have some left over—"

The twins immediately shook their heads and said no thanks. Jeremy grinned. His friends loved meat as much as he did.

"We're stuffed, Aunt Essie," Alex said quickly. "We had a huge dinner, didn't we Al?"

"Sure did. Mr. Taylor, can you give us a clue about what your new invention is?" Al asked, changing the subject.

Bob smiled. "Let's just say you will be impressed," he replied. "Hopefully!" he added with a self-deprecating chuckle.

"Did you finally convert the basement into a hologram movie theater?" Jeremy asked, hopefully.

"No, son, it's nothing like that. Nice try, though."

"I'd say it's a hybrid of things," Bob continued. "That's all the information you'll get out of me until Rob gets here. He's actually done some important work on the project as well," Bob added. "I wanted him to be here for the grand unveiling."

Rob Hart had been Bob's best friend since the seventh grade. They both worked at Human-istic Ltd., a company devoted to the creation of robots for all walks of life. Bob was a scientist by trade, while Rob was more on the technical side of the business. While Bob's persona was kind of nerdy, Rob was more the popular, extroverted guy on the corporate campus. Back in their school days, Rob had usually gotten the girls—except for Suzanne, who had been attracted to Bob from the beginning. They had met in college in Bob's sophomore year and been married several years later. Bob and Suzanne had been married for nineteen years. Their marriage, Bob thought, had been like a fairytale.

Suzanne had been a wonderful wife and mother, doting on Jeremy from the moment of his birth. Unfortunately, she had succumbed to cancer just last year, and Bob was understandably heartbroken. He had thrown himself into his work and into the basement project that took up most of his time when he wasn't at work.

"Botty," Aunt Essie said expectantly. "Can you please serve us all some cake? Al and Alex, you'll at least have some dessert, won't you?"

This time the twins smiled and nodded enthusiastically.

The robot cut the cake and served them each a piece in the living room. "Milk?" he asked.

"Yes, Botty," Bob said. "Milks all around!"

Maybe Dad will have more time for me now that his project is done, Jeremy thought hopefully as he took a bite of the carob cake.

"Are you okay, Jeremy?" Aunt Essie asked when he started to cough.

"Food's just gone down the wrong pipe," Jeremy lied. He didn't want his aunt to know that the cake was a little dry. "Dad, is your surprise something you are going to sell at Human-istic?" he wondered out loud.

"Son, this invention is for *you*!" Bob answered. "You are going to love it, Jeremy, I just know it!" When Bob got excited his ears turned pink, and they were turning bright pink now.

"I—I hope so, Dad."

A little while later, the doorbell rang. Bob went to the door. It was Rob. "Hey, buddy," Rob said, shaking Bob's hand. "Have you shown our little secret to Jeremy yet?"

"Not yet," Bob replied, motioning for Rob to enter. "We were waiting for you. We didn't want you to miss this."

"I bet the suspense is killing them," Rob said with a mischievous grin.

"Hi, Rob," Aunt Essie greeted him as she sailed into the living room. "Won't you have a seat?" Rob took one look at Essie, and his grin blossomed into a brilliant smile.

"Essie, it's great to see you," Rob remarked somewhat shyly. "You are as pretty as ever," he added.

Essie blushed. "Rob, you are such a flirt—and don't ever stop!"

"Hi, Alex, Al," Rob said, taking a seat near the twins.

"Hi, Mr. Hart," Al and Alex replied in unison.

"Mr. Hart, it is good to see you again. Would you like some cake?" Botty asked, walking in his general direction. "It is carob. Your favorite, I believe, sir."

"Thanks, Botty," Rob responded happily. "I'd love some!"

Essie blushed at his enthusiasm.

"Mr. Taylor," Alex chimed in excitedly. "Can we see the surprise now?"

"I think that can be arranged, Alex. I think *you* enjoy learning about my little science projects more than anyone else," Bob added, smiling.

"Yeah, she does," Al added. "Don't know where she gets it from." He shook his head. *"I'm* sure not into that stuff."

"Yeah," Jeremy said, smiling. "They're the nerds, and we're the cool race-car guys. No similarities there. Go figure!"

"Okay," Bob replied, getting up from his chair. "Rob, come with me." They descended into the basement. After several minutes, Rob came up the steps.

"Ladies and gentlemen, may I present to you Mr. Addison Taylor." Up the steps and out into the living room walked a young man with piercing blue eyes. Bob followed.

"Dad," Jeremy asked, looking at Addison, who was looking back at him and smiling. "Dad, who *is* this?" He watched Bob put his arm warmly around Addison's shoulders.

"This, my dear Jeremy, is your brand-new brother!" Bob said triumphantly.

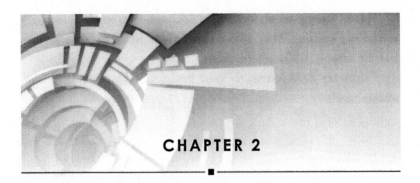

CHAPTER 2

■

SHOCK AND... SAY WHAT?

J eremy stared at the young man standing in front of him, his mouth agape. He didn't know how to respond to his father's assertion that this person was his brother. Jeremy was speechless.

Just then, Sammy came running up to Addison, growling menacingly at the young man. Essie grabbed him by the collar and led him away, muttering "That's not nice!" under her breath, and put Sammy safely away into his crate in the kitchen. She then joined the others in the living room.

"But Dad—I've never seen him before! Dad, were you married before you met Mom? What—what's going on?" Jeremy was exasperated.

"No, son." Bob laughed. "You know the only romantic relationship I've ever had was with your mother," he replied. "Guess again."

Jeremy looked closely at the good-looking young man standing in the middle of the floor. He didn't look anything like Jeremy, who was short and had wiry brown hair and green eyes. Addison was exceptionally handsome, and he had some physical qualities that reminded Jeremy of his dad, except Addison looked to be in his late teens or early twenties. He had blond, straight hair and blue eyes, and he was tall and muscular.

This guy could probably get any girl he wanted, Jeremy surmised silently. His heart sank. *Great—I've got another guy to compete with— except I can't compete with this*, he thought sadly.

Addison's face was handsome, his jawline chiseled. Girls loved that, Jeremy knew. All he had to do was look at Alex and Aunt Essie. They were practically swooning! Alex batted her eyes at him. Aunt Essie blushed. Jeremy was aggravated.

"Okay, Dad, I give up," Jeremy said. "I have no idea who this is . . ."

"Jeremy," Rob said, "Addison is a humanoid; he's actually a cyborg. He's got human DNA and my programming—with some robotics thrown in." He grinned. Rob's deep blue-gray eyes were shining as he spoke. He ran his fingers unconsciously through his wavy, sandy-brown hair. "Isn't he amazing?" he finished.

"Yes," Bob agreed. "He's part human clone and part machine. Addison is top-notch," he stated proudly.

"I'll say," Aunt Essie and Alex said simultaneously. They looked at one another and laughed.

"Jeremy, your dad put a lot of himself into Addison. He did most of the work on him," Rob said, patting the cyborg on the back.

"We feel like new parents," Bob added excitedly. "Jeremy, I made him for you. I wanted you to have a big brother—someone who'll always be there, someone who'll always have your back."

"Dad," Jeremy replied. "I have you. I have Aunt Essie—"

"But we're mortals," Bob said thoughtfully. "We can die . . ." His voice trailed off.

"Speak for *yourself*," Aunt Essie said, breaking the tension. Everyone laughed.

"Okay, *I* can die," Bob retorted. "Look what happened to your mother, Jeremy. If death can find her, it can—and will—find me, someday. I don't want you to be all alone," Bob said, staring at his shoes. "I wouldn't wish that on you, son. I wouldn't wish that on anybody."

Just then, Addison spoke up. "Hi, Jeremy. I'm very excited to finally meet you." Addison held out his hand. Jeremy took it, tentatively, and they shook hands. Jeremy was not sure about this guy. What was his dad thinking? *Geez.*

"See, Jeremy?" Rob said, smiling. "He likes you. He wants to be your friend."

"I'm Alex," Alex said happily, shaking Addison's hand. "I live two houses down. Al's my twin brother" she said, motioning with her head in the general direction of her brother. "We've been friends of Jeremy's for a long time."

"Nice to meet you," Addison replied, smiling. "Jeremy's very lucky to have a beautiful friend such as you."

Alex giggled and blushed. "You think I'm pretty?"

Jeremy rolled his eyes. *Here we go*, he thought.

"Please, sit down, Addison," Aunt Essie said, pointing to a cushy chair in the corner of the room. "That one's the most comfortable," she added, smiling.

"Don't mind if I do, Miss . . ."

"You can call me Aunt Essie," Essie replied. "That's what Jeremy calls me."

"Thank you, Aunt Essie," Addison said, his blue eyes shining.

"Think nothing of it," Essie said. "You are part of the family now, Addison. If you need anything—anything at all—just ask."

"I will. Thanks again." Addison sat down.

"Well, now that we've all met, does anyone have any questions?" Bob asked, settling into the couch.

"Yeah, I do," Al replied. "So Addison is a cyborg—"

"Yes," Bob replied, "but I think of him as becoming one of the family. He's human too, only better."

"Yes," Rob added. "He's got essentially a replica of a human brain, but Addison's brain also has a computer chip embedded in it. I've downloaded into him all of the knowledge we humans have gleaned from the beginning of time as we know it. Addison's brain has instantaneous access to that knowledge. He can also download new information off the Internet."

"Can he think for himself, Mr. Taylor?" asked Alex.

"Oh yes, he can, Alex. He's his own man," Rob retorted, patting Addison on the back.

"How about strength?" wondered Essie. "Can he help me move the furniture around?"

"He can do that and lots more," responded Bob, smiling.

"Aunt Essie, I hear you are a wonderful cook," Addison said. "I would love to learn. Can you teach me? I love the taste of excellent food."

"I'd be happy to," Essie replied, enjoying the praise for her contribution to the family.

"And I have been studying yoga," Addison added. "I know you teach it. Maybe I can join in a lesson?"

"Why, that would be wonderful!" Essie responded. "I'm so glad that you are interested in it."

"Of course I am, Aunt Essie. I know that's what keeps the body healthy and the mind strong."

Jeremy winced. *Just great,* he thought. He'd never shown any interest in his aunt's passions, and now this cyborg was showing him up.

"Well, I think Addison has made a friend here tonight," laughed Bob.

"I'll say," responded Aunt Essie. Everyone chuckled.

"Well, Mr. Taylor, he really *is* something, just like you said," Alex put in, getting up from the couch. "Al, we have to go now. I've got tons of homework, and I know you do too!" Al nodded in the affirmative and got up to leave. "It's been very nice meeting you, Addison," Alex added. "I'm sure we'll be seeing you around."

"Oh, you will," nodded Addison, smiling.

I'm sure he will too! thought Jeremy, somewhat peeved.

"Yeah, I should be going too," Rob agreed. "It's getting late." Bob and Jeremy walked their friends to the door and said good-bye.

"Dad, I want to take a walk—I'll be back soon." Jeremy needed some air. He could hardly breathe. He dutifully waved good-bye to his family and ran out the door and down the street at a brisk pace.

I have to get out of here! he thought, making his way several blocks to the little park nestled in the middle of the neighborhood. His mother used to take him there when he was little. They'd played a lot together in the sandbox with his little toy cars. The love of cars was something they had both had in common. It was getting dark, but Jeremy didn't care. He sat down on a picnic table bench and turned over the events of the evening in his mind. *Mom, I miss you . . . why did you have to die!* Jeremy held his head in his hands.

"Jeremy! Jeremy!" Someone in the distance was calling for him.

"Over here."

"Hi, Jeremy. Your dad and Aunt Essie want you to come home now. Are you okay?" It was Botty.

"I'm just missing my mom, Botty. And I'm not sure at all about Addison. What do you think? Do you like him?"

"I think he is nice." Botty sat down at the table across from Jeremy. "Your dad is a good inventor. You should come home now. Hop on my back, and I'll give you a ride home."

With that, the robot pushed the button on his side and transformed into a large, silver, streamlined motorcycle, his bright blue eyes now serving as headlights.

Jeremy reluctantly jumped onto the robot's back, revved the engine, and drove the robot home. His aunt was waiting for him on the front stoop. She smiled and waved as the two drove into the driveway.

"I was worried about you, Jeremy," she said, patting the porch step. "Come on, sit down next to me and tell me what's up." She then turned her attention to the robot. "Botty, thanks for bringing Jeremy home. You can go now."

Jeremy dutifully got off the robot/motorcycle and took a seat next to his aunt. The robot morphed back into his old self, acknowledged Aunt Essie, and walked past them into the house.

"So, tell me about it," Aunt Essie said, looking out into the darkness. "How are you feeling about what's happening here?"

Jeremy didn't know where to begin, so he just poured his feelings out. "I miss Mom," he started. "I know Dad wouldn't have made

Addison if she were still here. I just don't get why Dad did this—made a cyborg. We don't need someone else in the family."

"Your dad thinks you do. He worries. He wants you to have a brother."

"The guy's a cyborg, Aunt Essie. No offense, but I don't really think you can make a brother out of things. Brothers of humans ought to be born, not made."

"That couldn't happen, Jeremy."

"Dad could adopt."

"He didn't want to. He wanted to create the perfect brother for you. Jeremy, I know this is hard for you, but give Addison a chance, at least. For your father. What do you say?"

"Well... I guess..."

"Come on, let's go inside."

They both got up and went into the kitchen, where Bob and Addison were just finishing the dishes.

"Hi, Jeremy! Glad you're back. Did you have a nice walk?" Bob wanted to know.

"Yeah."

"That's good."

"Dad, um, where'll Addison be sleeping?" Jeremy was curious.

"Well, son, I thought he would sleep in your room. You have that extra bed in there that we set up for Al when he sleeps over, and it's a pretty large room. That way, you two can become acquainted that much sooner!" Bob was obviously excited, hoping Jeremy and Addison would become close fast.

"Well, I guess..."

"Great! Then it's settled. Addison, Jeremy will show you to your new room. Tomorrow Essie will take you shopping for some clothes. If that's all right with you, Essie?"

"Of course it's okay," responded Essie. "I've got some time to do it in the morning. It'll be fun, won't it, Addison?"

"You bet, Aunt Essie. I'm looking forward to it!"

Jeremy decided it was getting late himself. He said good night to his dad and aunt and then shepherded his new "brother" up the stairs to his bedroom.

"This'll be yours," he said, pointing to the bed across from his.

"Thanks, Jeremy. This is great. I know we'll get on together. Thanks for sharing your bedroom with me."

"No sweat," Jeremy replied, pulling off his jeans and grabbing a white T-shirt and plaid boxers. Pointing at his sleeping attire, he motioned to his new roommate and asked, "You want a pair?"

"No thanks. I won't need them, because I'm hot," Addison replied.

"Oh no you don't, dude!" Jeremy shrieked, alarmed.

"What? What do you mean? I don't need clothes to sleep in tonight," Addison said, looking confused. "It's sweltering in here."

"Look, Addison. Guys who're friends don't sleep together in the same room without a T-shirt and boxers, you know? They just don't! It's just common sense!"

"Jeremy, I don't know what you're talking about. I'm just hot. Doesn't it make more sense for me to go without clothes?" Addison looked quizzically at his new brother.

"Look, dude, that's *not* how it works." Jeremy grabbed a T-shirt and pair of boxers and threw them in the general vicinity of Addison. "Take these, dude, and *wear* them. If you're living in my room, you gotta play by my rules. T-shirts and boxers every night, every time. Hot or not. Get it?"

"Got it."

"Good." *Guess the cyborg's not so perfect after all,* Jeremy thought, smiling to himself.

Addison dutifully put on the bright-red boxers and T-shirt that Jeremy had thrown at him and slipped between the covers of his new bed. He lay down, smiling. "I'm so happy I'm your new brother, Jeremy," he said. "I want you to like me."

"Sure, whatever. I like you fine, Addison. Now just go to sleep, okay?" Jeremy switched off the light between the beds. He got into his own pajamas and then into bed. He covered his head with his blanket. Jeremy was completely floored by what his dad had created. *I can't think about this now*, he thought. He felt extremely tired and overwhelmed. Soon both boys were sleeping soundly.

CHAPTER 3

■

MONEY, MONEY, MONEY

The next morning at work, Bob was drinking his first cup of coffee and checking his e-mail when Rob came into his office and shut the door. "Bob," he said pointedly, "that cyborg you and I created is just so amazing. The work we put into it definitely paid off. I was thinking that we should tell Vladimir about him. I'm sure he would be interested." Vladimir Petrov was the CEO of Human-istic Ltd., where Bob and Rob had worked since getting out of grad school back in the '90s. Human-istic made robots of all shapes and sizes and cloned human organs for transplants.

"You know, Robert," Bob said tersely, looking up from his computer, "I think of Addison as a son, not a commodity."

"I know, I know," Rob said. "I am not saying that we would sell Addison per se, just the new technology that we've created off-site. I know there must be tons of people who would want to have a cyborg like him at home, helping out around the house, or to be like a son or daughter to them, as opposed to a robot: metallic and computerlike. You could help thousands of people who have lost someone or who couldn't have a child of their own, have a special person in their lives." Rob sat back in his seat, waiting for Bob to respond.

"Well," Bob said slowly, "when you put it that way . . ."

"Yes! I knew you'd see my point." Rob smiled. "Let's set up a meeting with Vladimir. It can't hurt to talk—right, old friend?"

"Okay," Bob agreed. "Let's talk this thing through and see what we might be able to do with this technology."

"Great! Bob, I already set up the meeting for later this afternoon, at four o'clock. I knew you'd see things my way. We'll be meeting in Vladimir's office. See you later, buddy!" Rob got up and left with a jaunty wave. Bob sighed. Rob had always been the one who did things spontaneously—and often prior to getting approval. He was not surprised that Rob had already set up the meeting. He also knew that Rob was hoping to make a ton of money from their invention.

Bob, however, was not motivated by money, and Rob knew that. Rob also knew that Bob would do anything to help someone else and that if he put a slant on the concept of utilizing the software for the good of humanity, then Bob would sign on.

I'll have to see what Vladimir says before I decide whether I want to share the new technology with the world, thought Bob. If Vladimir was only motivated by the bottom line on this, Bob decided, then he would not agree to sell.

After school later that same day, Al, Alex, and Jeremy decided to go to the local burger shop for some snacks. "Oh, this burger is so-o-o good!" Jeremy said passionately as he took another large bite.

"You know, Jeremy, I think you like meat a little too much!" Al took a sip of his milkshake. "I mean, the way you carry on about it—it's kind of . . . um . . . weird, dude!"

"I know—but I just love steak, you know? And chicken and pork and other meats too! Aunt Essie says it's bad for me, and she won't serve it at home. The only way I can get it is to go out for food!"

"Well, Jeremy, I'm happy to come with you for a burger anytime! You know that about me," Al said, smiling and taking a big bite of his own burger.

"I think you both sound stupid when you talk about food," Alex chimed in. "I mean, it's just food!"

19

The guys were completely taken aback. "Sis, you just don't understand," Al replied. "A hamburger is like the food of the gods!"

"Aunt Essie would have a fit if she could see us now," Jeremy said, grinning. "But I have to say there's only so much tofu I can take! She means well, though, and I know she has Dad's and my best interests at heart."

"She's pretty awesome," Alex replied. "I think she's really sweet, her obsession with all things soy notwithstanding. Just direct her to some less "soy-tastic" recipes and you'll live to see age eighteen. By the way, how did things go with Addison last night?"

"Oh, fine." Jeremy did his best to hide his disappointment over his dad's gift.

"Don't you like Addison?" asked Alex. "You don't sound too enthused."

Jeremy had never been able to hide his feelings from Alex, even when they were little. "Um, he's okay," Jeremy muttered.

"Well, I don't know if I'd like it much if our dad came home with a smart, good-looking guy and told me I needed to treat him like my brother," Al stated. "It's hard enough to make it in this world competing against *people*," he continued. "Now we have to compete against cyborgs who have brains coming out the wazoo and are built like Brad Pitt? Geez, Jeremy, what a bummer. No offense."

"None taken," Jeremy replied, looking a bit depressed.

After they finished their food, Jeremy dropped Al and Alex at their place and continued home himself. He parked his beloved Mustang and gave it a pat before opening the door from the garage to the kitchen. He heard New Age music coming from the living room. *Aunt Essie is teaching her yoga class*, he thought. He entered the living room, where ten women were standing in their leotards, stretching their hands up above their heads. Addison was standing next to Aunt Essie.

"Addison, dear, can you show the ladies how best to reach for the floor," Essie asked, smiling.

"Of course," Addison replied. "Ladies, gently bend over from your waist, and slowly reach your fingers toward your toes . . . like this!" he said, turning around and reaching for his toes.

The ladies sighed, much as Aunt Essie and Alex had the night before when they'd met Addison. One lady in her forties said to her friend standing next to her, "He's gorgeous, don't you think?"

"We heard that, Amanda," Essie said, at which everyone laughed.

"Well, he is!" Amanda said insistently.

"We know!" All of the ladies responded in the affirmative.

Addison turned around with a grin on his face. "Well, I think you ladies are all beautiful yourselves," he said, looking out over the sea of smiling faces in the group.

"You do?" Amanda asked.

"Absolutely," Addison replied. He took her hand in his, looked into her eyes, and said, "Amanda, you are beautiful, and don't let anyone convince you otherwise. You are a wonderful woman."

Amanda had not heard a man say anything like that to her in years. "I think I love you, Addison!" she said, playfully.

Just then, Jeremy cleared his throat. "Oh! Hi, Jeremy," Aunt Essie said, turning toward him. "I'm sorry; I didn't see you there. I hope you haven't been there long."

"No, not long. I think I'll go upstairs to study."

"Jeremy, let me know if you need any help," Addison said. "I hear math and science are not your strongest subjects."

"Oh, I'm okay with them," Jeremy replied. "I think I'll be fine." With that, he went upstairs to his room. *Great*, he thought as he took his books out of his backpack. *The guy is great at math and science— unlike me. Dad must love that about him.* Jeremy's math homework involved calculus, and he had absolutely no idea how to answer the questions he had, but he was hell-bent on not asking Addison for help. *I'd rather fail*, he groused, twirling his pencil between his fingers.

Back at Human-istic, Bob and Rob were waiting in CEO Vladimir Petrov's office for him to return. The office was spectacular, as far as offices go. It was all clear glass and blue Formica throughout, with modern-looking, angular furniture and a view that wouldn't quit—the city of San Jose spread out for miles and miles.

A few minutes later, Vladimir entered the room. "Hi, Bob, Rob," he said, closing the door behind him. "Hope you weren't waiting long."

"No, not at all," Bob responded. "We just got here."

"Great. I hear you may have a proposition for me," Vladimir said, taking his seat at his desk. Bob and Rob were seated on the other side of his humongous, forbidding glass desktop. There was an hourglass sitting near Vladimir's right side. "Do you like it?" Vladimir asked, pointing to the glass. "I got it to keep me from running too long at meetings. Time is money, right?" He turned the hourglass over.

"Absolutely, Vladimir," Rob agreed. "So, let's get right to this. We invented a cyborg. I think you'll be very interested in him as a model for a possible product line for the firm," he continued. "Not only is he made up of human DNA, he also has the ability to think for himself—extrapolate, if you will, thoughts and ideas that are presented to him. He's got a computer chip inside his brain that gives him the option of searching a database for knowledge of any kind to help him with his tasks. He's strong and built to last, with lots of reinforcement in the extremities," Rob finished excitedly.

"Yes," Vladimir replied, cutting him off. "Bob, did you and Rob do this whole project outside of work, with your own resources?"

"We did. We used the funds from the bonuses you gave us for the last robotics project we worked on."

"Right. Got it. Understood. So, this new hybrid technology is something you think Human-istic might be able to utilize?" Vladimir changed the subject, staring laser-like into Bob's eyes. Vladimir could read people like nobody's business. It was a little intimidating for Bob.

"Yes, absolutely, Vladimir. Rob reminded me that there are many people in the world who have a need for a friend, or who have lost a family member, who could benefit from this work."

"Perhaps," Vladimir replied. "Can I meet this Addison and see for myself?"

"Sure!" Rob blurted out. "I mean, what about it, Bob?"

"Don't see why not," Bob said dispassionately.

"Great!" Vladimir was showing a bit of enthusiasm. "Let's all meet for dinner. Tomorrow night at Mario's? Around six?"

"We'll see you then!" Rob replied.

"I guess that'll work," Bob agreed.

"Well, time's up," Vladimir said with a grin as he observed the last grain of sand fall in his hourglass. "See you tomorrow night." Bob and Rob got up, and each shook Vladimir's hand.

"We'll see you then," Rob nodded.

As they left the office, Rob was nearly walking on air. "Did you see?" he exclaimed. "Vladimir is very interested in Addison—I mean, our technology. I know when he meets him, he'll be chomping at the bit, you know?" Rob was so excited he was hardly able to keep himself from jumping up and down. Back in the day when they'd been kids, Bob thought, he *would* have jumped up and down.

"Yep," Bob responded. "He's excited all right. Let's take this one step at a time, though, Rob," he urged. "There may not be a fit between this technology and Human-istic. Let's just wait and see."

"No fit!" Rob couldn't believe his ears. "Of course there's a fit! You know what? I have a feeling we're gonna become rich, Bob—*rich*!"

"Rob, Rob, one step at a time, buddy, okay? You're getting a bit ahead of yourself again."

"Yeah, okay," Rob agreed dejectedly. "You never get excited, do you, Bob?"

"Yes, I do, but I just need—oh, I don't know—an actual *offer* to make me excited."

"Offer, schmoffer. You'll see," Rob said, getting into his car. "Everything's gonna work out great!"

"Bye, Rob!" Bob said with a laugh. He got into his green Tesla electric sports car and then headed off for home.

CHAPTER 4

■

GREEN WITH ENVY

B ob was pulling into the driveway as Aunt Essie, Jeremy, and
Addison were just sitting down to a meal of fried artichokes and
rice. "Hi, Dad!" Jeremy greeted him as he entered the kitchen.

"Hey, kids. Essie," Bob replied, closing the door behind him. "I see
I'm just in time for dinner."

"Yes you are, Dad," Addison agreed, pulling out the chair next to
him so Bob could sit down. "Have a seat."

"So, what's new, family?" Bob asked while Botty brought him a
plate, silverware, and a glass of water.

"Well," Aunt Essie replied, "Addison helped me with my yoga class
today, and he was a real hit with the ladies."

"Yeah," Jeremy chimed in. "They really seemed to like him—*a lot!*"

"They were all very nice," Addison agreed, grinning.

"That's an understatement," Aunt Essie said, smiling. "They *loved*
you, Addison—especially Amanda!"

"Wow, what a great first impression you made, Addy," Bob replied,
smiling too. "Guess you won't have any problem finding dates. But who
is Amanda?"

Addy? thought Jeremy, looking at his dad in disbelief. *Okay, that's
an interesting nickname.*

"Amanda is one of my best students," Essie replied, taking a bite of artichoke. "She's a bit older than Addy, but so what? You know, Addison, you could probably learn a thing or two from her . . ."

"So, did you two find some nice clothes for Addison?" Bob asked, changing the subject and motioning toward Essie.

"Yes, we did, but there were actually three of us on the shopping spree," Essie replied, taking a drink of water. "We brought Botty with us, right Botty?"

"Yes, Ms. Essie. I had fun with you and Addison today. I like clothes shopping," Botty said while he served Bob his meal. "Everything Addison tried on fit him perfectly."

Of course it did, thought Jeremy irritably as he eyed the carob brownies intended for dessert.

"And everything looked great on him!" Aunt Essie added, swooning in Addison's direction.

"We had a hard time choosing what to buy," Addison said, putting down his water glass. "But I think we did a pretty good job, don't you think, Aunt Essie?"

"I do. We got tons of great-looking clothes for you, didn't we? What do you think, Bob?" Aunt Essie asked. "Right now, he's wearing Ralph Lauren—a pair of blue jeans and a great button-down brown shirt, for everyday wear, right? We got this outfit and everything at the stores in the Gilroy Outlets. Addy, get up and model it for your dad and Jeremy."

Yes, please do. Jeremy rolled his eyes and pushed himself away from the table. Suddenly the carob brownies seemed less appealing. While Addison and Essie continued their pretend modeling show, Jeremy quietly excused himself. He went upstairs to his room, took out his math book, and sat down at his desk to study. *Anything* was better than witnessing that ridiculous parody going on downstairs. If one more person complimented Addison on how handsome he was, Jeremy was going to puke. He needed to get his mind off his new "brother" and on to something else. Even math was a welcome distraction.

After a while, Jeremy's dad came upstairs to check up on him. "Come in," Jeremy responded to the gentle knocks. He laid his book aside and looked up to see his dad entering his room.

"Hi, son. Working on your homework?" Bob asked with a grin when his eyes alighted on the discarded textbook. "That's great. You know, if you need help with your math, Addy can help—"

"Yeah, Dad, I'm aware. Thanks."

"Jeremy, is something bothering you?"

"Dad, no, I'm fine. It's just that little modeling deal they were doing downstairs . . . it was making me kinda nauseous. I mean, I get it that Addison is great-looking, all right? He doesn't have to flaunt it, you know?"

Bob laughed. "I think Aunt Essie has a little crush on him, don't you?"

"She and every other woman that sees him! Honestly, Dad, did you have to make him look like some modern Adonis? What's wrong with him looking a little more . . . like me?" Jeremy asked, finally saying what had been on his mind since he'd first been introduced to Addison.

"Wow, son—you know, that didn't even enter my mind. I just wanted to make him the best he could be, and that included his looks, I guess. But you know, Jeremy, I made you better . . . because I made you with your wonderful mom, right? Always remember that." Bob put his arm around his son's shoulders. "And always remember that I love you—you are my number-one son!" Bob said as he pressed a soothing kiss to Jeremy's forehead. "Oh, yeah, I wanted to let you know we're going out to dinner with Vladimir and Rob tomorrow night. So keep the date open for us, okay?"

"Sure, Dad," Jeremy replied. "And Dad? Thanks. I love you too."

"I know, son. Study hard."

After Bob left the room, Jeremy sighed. His dad always seemed to know exactly what to say to make him feel better. He reviewed the conversation he'd just had with his dad and realized that he really had a great relationship with his father. Jeremy felt as if he were the luckiest son alive. But he also knew he'd have to find a way to accept Addison into his life—if only for his dad's sake.

CHAPTER 5

■

SIGN HERE!

T he next evening, Bob, Rob, Jeremy, Aunt Essie and Addison were seated at a quiet table at Mario's Ristorante, waiting for Vladimir to arrive. They found themselves in turn enjoying a piece of newly baked bread, which they dipped in a small bowl of olive oil and fresh garlic that sat in the middle of the table. "Man, this is good," exclaimed Jeremy. The rest nodded in agreement as they ate.

Mario's was almost everyone's favorite Italian restaurant in Gilroy, partially because the owners and staff used fresh ingredients. The food served there generally incorporated lots of fresh, locally grown garlic, and the patrons appreciated the intense flavor and pungent aroma that the garlic provided. In fact, Gilroyans grew so much garlic that the town was known everywhere as the "Garlic Capital of the World." At least it was in California.

Rob and the Taylors were all perusing their menus when Vladimir and another gentleman, dressed in a nicely tailored blue suit, entered the restaurant. "Hi, everyone," Vladimir exclaimed, taking a seat at the table. "Garcon, we'll need another chair." Vladimir motioned to the waiter, who immediately pulled a chair over to the table and then grabbed a table setting from a nearby table and placed it in front of Vladimir's guest. "I thought I would bring Dave Rose along," Vladimir said, looking over at Dave, "in case we decide to do a deal. He's our lead lawyer when it comes to our technical acquisitions." Vladimir smiled.

"We're happy you could come, Dave," Bob said, greeting him with a polite nod in his general direction. "You already know Rob," Bob said slowly, "but I'd like you to meet my sons. This is Jeremy . . . and this is the man of the hour, Addison." The boys shook Dave's hand. "And this is my sister, Essie," Bob stated, motioning toward her. "She's the soul of the family," he finished.

"Nice to meet you, Essie," Dave responded, shaking her hand. "In fact, it's nice to meet all of you," Dave said with a curt nod. "And it sounds like Addison, here, may become not only a beloved family member but, technologically, a great asset to Human-istic."

"I think so," Vladimir replied. "But let's order before we get into business issues. I'm starved." Everyone agreed with Vladimir, and a waiter was called over to take their orders.

Once the server had jotted down their orders in his book and left their table with a slight bow, Vladimir focused his attention back to the task at hand. "So, Rob, tell us about the technology you used in creating Addison."

"Well, he's very special, as you can see," Rob began. "We cloned most of his organs and skin from donated tissues, and we made his face by grafting the skin onto a premade mold."

"He's one nice specimen, don't you think?" Bob added proudly. "We took special care to make him appealing to the eye."

"What do you mean by 'nice specimen,' Dad?" Addison asked quizzically.

Everyone laughed, while Aunt Essie explained that it was his handsome appearance that made him a "nice specimen"—and also so attractive to women.

"And, Addy," Essie continued, "not only are you a godlike creature, but you are not conceited about it. Stay that way!"

"Yes, Addison, *please* stay that way," Jeremy chimed in, rolling his eyes. Everyone laughed.

Bob glanced over at Jeremy, wondering what that comment was all about. Then he went on to explain how Addison's brain worked and how he had a supercomputer inside that was at his disposal anytime he needed it.

"Rob really outdid himself with the software," Bob said, looking admiringly at his friend. "You know, Vladimir, Rob made Addison practically the most knowledgeable cyborg on the planet. I have to hand it to him."

"Aw, thanks, buddy," Rob said, lightly punching his friend in the arm. "But this whole concept and overall design came from you, so I'd have to say you're not so bad in the brain department yourself."

"Okay, that's enough self-deprecation, guys. It's making me a little nauseous," Vladimir said while holding his throat as though he were choking. "Let's discuss terms. I know Human-istic, and the public at large, can benefit from your work."

"Um, give us a minute here, Vladimir," Bob replied. "This is all happening a little too quickly. Rob, can I see you at the bar for a minute?"

Rob nodded, and as the two of them walked into the bar area, they heard Vladimir reply, "Don't take too long, boys. This offer isn't good forever."

Rob and Bob sat down at the bar. Their heads were spinning. "Is this *really* gonna happen?" Bob asked, looking somewhat blown away.

"Yeah, isn't this great?" Rob answered, smiling broadly. "Bob, this is so cool!"

"But really, Rob, is this whole thing gonna go well? I mean, is creating a bunch of brilliant cyborgs in the best interests of society?" Bob wasn't so sure.

"Society!" Rob said loudly. "Society will be thrilled! Just think! People can get all the answers to questions that come up by just asking their very own cyborg. How great will that be?"

"Well, I guess . . ."

"You guess? You should know! You know how great it is for you to have Addison as part of your family. Don't you want everyone to feel the same way you do?" Rob asked incredulously.

"But how do we know that everyone has the same ideas for the cyborgs that we do?" Bob countered. "They could be used for good, but they could also be used for evil."

"That's true of every new invention," Rob replied. "By your line of thinking, no one would ever invent anything new, because it could be used for evil. We'd still be in the stone age if people thought that way."

"Point taken, Rob," Bob replied. "But do you think Vladimir will utilize the plans for the cyborg for the good of mankind? He is a little on the . . . well, you know, on the greedy side."

"He knows how you feel about Addison and how you see the production of the cyborgs being utilized," Rob said slowly. "He has great admiration for you and your wishes. He wants to keep you on board with the organization. I can't believe he'd do anything to jeopardize losing you."

"I guess . . ."

"I know!" Rob finished. "He's a good guy, Bob. We've known him for years. You don't have to worry about Vladimir!"

"You have no reservations, Rob? Should we talk to a lawyer about this?"

"Actually, I had Legal forward a copy of the contract to my lawyer, Chad, this afternoon. He says it's fine. It's boilerplate. But we are giving Vladimir all of the rights to Addison's design. If, for some reason, he doesn't get a copy of our cyborg plans, then he can take possession of Addison, and reverse-engineer him, if need be."

"That won't happen," Bob countered. "I've got it all, right up here."

"You don't have the plans in a database somewhere?" Rob countered, somewhat concerned.

"I have the plans, Rob. But they're somewhat scattered around a bit. I need to pull them together into one cohesive document, that's all."

"So, do you want to go forward with this?" Rob asked hesitantly. "I can tell you I have my piece—the brain-chip plans—in a document, ready for Vladimir. I'm ready to go on my end. Chad says we both stand to become actual billionaires from this deal. Can you believe it? <u>Us</u>?" Rob shook his head.

"Not really," Bob said, smiling broadly. "But think of what we can do with that kind of money. Maybe even cure cancer." Bob was already planning his next experiment to find a cure for the disease.

"Shall we go back and sign the contract, Bob?"

"Yes, buddy. Let's go get this done."

The two men shook hands and then got up from the bar and went back to their party, who were waiting with bated breath for the outcome of their discussion.

"Well," Dave asked, waving the document in front of the inventors, "what's the verdict? Are you two ready to sign?"

"Give us your pen, Dave," Rob said, grinning broadly. "Yes, we're ready." Everyone at the table clapped.

"All right, guys!" Vladimir said excitedly, rubbing his hands together. "We've got a deal!"

"Yes, we do," Bob murmured, somewhat dazed and surprised at the speediness with which the deal was put together. "I really wasn't sure this was going to happen tonight. This was much easier and cleaner than I thought it would be."

"That's because we have a great lawyer like Dave working for us," Vladimir replied, clapping a hand on Dave's shoulder and giving it a playful shake.

"Thank you, Vladimir," Dave said with a stiff smile and a surreptitious tug to straighten out his rumpled jacket. "But I'm just the intermediary here. So, what are the next steps you'd like to see?"

"Well, I'd like to know when I can expect the plans for the cyborg—can you give me a time frame?" Vladimir asked in a serious tone.

"It'll take me a while to combine Rob's work with mine and get you one detailed document," Bob responded. "I think I can have everything to you by the end of August. How about the twenty-fifth? That way you can start production first thing in September."

"Sounds great, Bob. That works for me." Vladimir was satisfied. September had been the month he had already designated as the time to begin the production of the cyborgs. He had already lined up some tentative orders for several clients, including the US Army, though Rob and Bob had not been told about this turn of events.

With coffee finished, Vladimir picked up the tab for the evening. "Glad we could make a deal, Rob, Bob. See you both Monday," Vladimir said as he and Dave got up from the table to leave. "Take good care of Addison. He and his kind may be our company's future!"

"We will. See you Monday, Vladimir," Bob replied while waving good-bye to his boss. Everyone else at the table said their good-byes as well.

After Vladimir and Dave had left, Bob and Rob looked at each other and grabbed each other's shoulders in excitement. "We did it!" Rob exclaimed, laughing and jubilant.

"I know!" Bob grinned. "This is unbelievable!"

"Yes, you two are so-o-o awesome," Aunt Essie exclaimed, obviously joking. "Just don't let all this success go to your heads."

"Dad?" Jeremy asked, checking his watch. "I've got to study for finals tomorrow, so can we leave now?"

"Of course, son," Bob answered with a smile. "Let's go."

As they all got up from the table to head home, they were feeling happy and satisfied. But all of them also knew inside that things would never be the same again.

Later that evening, Alex and Al stopped by Jeremy's house to find out how things had gone at the restaurant. Everyone was sitting in the living room having some herbal tea that Essie had made.

"So, Addy," Alexandra began, picking up his hand and looking into his eyes. "Did you 'wow' them?"

"I don't know about that, but I guess Vladimir thought my prototype was marketable—you know, that if they made more of me they could make a decent profit."

"They thought more than that, Alex," Bob insisted. "Addison is one-of-a-kind, but the general technology that we sold to Humanistic is a mix of technologies that, taken together, can create the most humanistic invention ever seen on the planet."

Botty entered the room to offer everyone some cookies to go with their tea. "Is Addison different from me, Mr. Taylor?" Botty wanted to know. "Or is he the same?"

"Botty, he is both. He's part robot and part human. He has human DNA, and you do not. But he also has a combination of technologies inherent in his makeup, so he is like you too. We call Addison 'cyborganic.'"

"Wow, that's cool, Dad," Jeremy chimed in. "Cyborganic—is the organic part of Addison special?"

"Sort of," Bob said thoughtfully. "Actually, Addy," he began, turning to the cyborg, "I added myself to the mix, if you will. I wasn't sure I should tell you . . ." Bob shifted uncomfortably in his chair. "But, anyway, you are a mix of technology and cloning using DNA—in your case, *my* DNA. It's a little unusual to utilize your own instead of an anonymous donor's, I must admit. But I wanted more than a cyborg—a being with super strength, intelligence, and humanity. I wanted a son—one that would be able to be a brother to Jeremy, here. I chose to ignore the rules, so to speak."

The entire room fell silent as each one individually processed this new revelation. Jeremy's eyes widened. He was completely shocked. "Dad, no!" Jeremy got up from his chair and ran upstairs to his room. He threw himself on the bed. "Dad's created a—a Frankenstein! I—I can't believe this!" He began to sob. *He betrayed me!* Jeremy was getting angry. *Why does he do this to me! I didn't want Addison to begin with! He'd rather be with him—he'd rather be a part of him! Well, I hate him—I hate them both!* Jeremy got up and locked his bedroom door. The last thing he needed now was to have a conversation with either his dad or Addison. He needed some time to be alone and to process the new information by himself.

Downstairs, the group decided that they'd leave Jeremy alone for a while to give him some time with his thoughts.

After an awkward period of silence, Addison spoke. "So Dad, I really *am* a part of the family," he said slowly, letting the new information sink in.

"That's right."

"So, let's get down to the most important thing," Al started hesitantly. "Don't you think you should've told Jeremy about this before now?"

"Al!" Alex cried in outrage, punching him in the side. "That's none of our business. It's just rude to ask."

"That's okay," Bob said worriedly. "I—I guess I should've, Al. It never occurred to me, to be honest. I just thought he'd love the idea of Addison as much as I did."

"Guess you were wrong." Al took a long breath and then continued, "What I really want to know is, how are you gonna square all this with Jeremy?"

"I guess I really made a mess of things."

"Bob, how could you!" Essie shook her head disapprovingly. "I think this is going to take a lot of getting used to, on Jeremy's part."

Bob fell silent. He was deep in thought.

The rest of the group grew increasingly uncomfortable. "Well, I guess we all should be going," Alex stated finally.

Aunt Essie escorted the group out the door and then came back inside to where Addison and her brother sat.

"You two have some things you'll have to work out with Jeremy," Essie stated emphatically. "His happiness has to come first, Bob. I hope he can find it in his heart to forgive you." With that she left the room, leaving Bob and Addison to their thoughts.

"I blew it, Addison," Bob finally stated, holding his head in his hands. "I wasn't thinking of Jeremy's feelings, if I'm honest. I was really thinking of my own. I missed Suzanne, and I guess I was looking to fill the void—with you. Sorry, Addison." Bob's eyes filled with tears.

"That's okay, Dad. If it weren't for you, I wouldn't be here. It doesn't matter to me what your motives were. The bottom line is that I'm here, and I'm glad. I am sorry for Jeremy, though. I hope in time that things will work themselves out."

"Yeah, I guess that's all either of us can hope for," Bob agreed. "He's a good kid. He knows my motives were good. I think if we just give him some space, he'll come around. At least, I hope he will."

CHAPTER 6

■

LET'S MOVE

Over the course of the next few weeks, Essie's yoga class grew so big, due to the popularity of Addison, that she needed to move to a dance studio to accommodate all of the new pupils that had signed up for her classes. The space at home had just become too "intimate." Essie discovered the perfect space, located in the center of downtown Gilroy, which lent itself well to both yoga and to foot traffic. It had a huge picture window that faced out into the street. *People will walk by and see us doing our class. It'll turn them on to what we do, and they'll want to be a part of it!* Essie was ecstatic. She decided to rent the studio right then and there.

Addison loved the yoga work and meeting all the women who seemed to enjoy the class. He had a great time with Aunt Essie too. Her engaging demeanor drew all kinds of people to her, and her classes included people from all walks of life. There was the nuclear physicist, Carmen, and the Mexican restaurant owner, Maria, as well as the homemaker, Shannon, all in the same class. Addison loved talking to Carmen about nuclear fusion and to Maria about great Mexican recipes. He was enjoying the diversity and loving every moment with the ladies, and it showed.

"Addy, do you know how to get dog urine out of a carpet?" asked Shannon, after a particularly grueling series of yoga poses including the Downward Dog. "This pose reminds me!"

"Of course, Shannon," Addison answered, smiling into her quizzical face. "The answer, my dear, is baking soda."

"Gosh, Addy, how did we ever get along without you?" Shannon countered, batting her long, black eyelashes at Addison.

"Yeah," Carmen agreed. "Who else can I talk to about nuclear issues around here? You're the man, Addy!"

"I'm gonna bring you some of my award-winning enchiladas. You're going to love them, I am sure!" chimed in Maria.

"Thanks a lot!" Addison said, grinning. "I love your food, Maria!"

On moving day, Essie and Addison toted all of the mats, balls, and other paraphernalia to the new, much-larger space. Then they put up a new black-and white-sign, which Essie had made, outside the doorway to the studio. It read "Yoga Classes for Life with Essie and Addison Taylor." They were in business.

"Aunt Essie, you didn't have to put my name on the sign," Addison told her after they had secured the sign tightly to the outer facade of the building.

"You're the reason we had to move to a larger location, Addy," Essie replied, smiling. "It's because of you that the attendance of my classes has tripled. I consider you my partner now," Essie finished. "That is, if you'd like to be. Will you be my partner, Addy?"

Addison was stunned. He'd only been working with Aunt Essie for a short time. He loved yoga, and he loved spending time with her too. She was always so nice, and she treated him well, as if he'd always been one of the family. "Sure, Aunt Essie, if you want me to. I'd love to be your partner."

"Then it's settled," Essie replied happily, giving Addison a hug. "We make a great team, don't we?"

"Yes, we do," Addy agreed, smiling. "We'll make this place the most popular yoga center ever!"

Just then the door opened. It was Amanda. "Hi, Addison, Essie," she cooed playfully as she sauntered into the center. "I wanted to be the first to wish you both well in your new venture."

"Thanks, Amanda," Addison replied. "We're looking forward to making this place a home away from home for you and the other students."

"For *me*?" Amanda asked, smiling shyly, looking wistfully into Addison's eyes.

"Well, for you, of course, and also for everyone else . . ."

"Sure, of course," Amanda replied, turning away to check out the new surroundings.

"So, you'll be at our first class here?" Essie asked. "Addison will be leading the first one at two this afternoon, while I take care of some business."

"Addison will be leading the class?" Amanda repeated, looking longingly into Addison's eyes. "Oh, I'll be there, for sure! See you later." Amanda waved good-bye as she left the store.

Aunt Essie laughed. "She really has a crush on you, Addy," she said, stating the obvious. "At least we can count on one very passionate and regular customer!"

"Yeah, I have a feeling we'll be see a lot of her," Addison agreed, with a sense of resignation. "I hope she's not one of those stalkers," he added.

"Don't worry; she's harmless. Just keep being nice to her. She loves the attention. I think she's kind of lonely, Addy."

"Of course. I'll keep her happy."

"I know you will. I'll see you later, Addy," Essie said, gathering up some paperwork from her desk and putting it into her briefcase. "I gotta go to the bank and take care of business. Hold down the fort for me, and I'll see you later."

Over a very short period of time, Addison had become involved in a variety of activities around Gilroy and had become pretty well known among the Gilroyans. Besides being popular with the yoga crowd, Addison had also become a virtual star on the basketball court in town. He excelled in sports, and the guys who were regulars at the court fought over which team he would be on. And usually that was the team that won the game.

Addison had also taken a part-time job as a guest professor at the local community college. He taught the Introduction to Biology class. "I love biology," he told his students. "It's what we're all about, right?"

Meanwhile, Bob and Essie had given Botty to Addison for transportation to and from his work and other activities. Addison loved driving the robot/motorcycle—he found it exhilarating. "You rock, you know that, Botty?" Addison exclaimed as the rode home from the college one evening.

"Thanks, Addison," Botty answered as they swerved back and forth around the sharp curves of the twisty country road. "I like going fast. This is fun for me!"

Bob was very proud of Addison's teaching skills. "Son, you have a gift. I love science, but I can't teach. You can!"

"Thanks, Dad. I like it too. The kids are remarkable, and they're fun to be around."

"You just enjoy yourself, okay, son?"

"Okay, I will, Dad."

Addison enjoyed all the various areas in life that he'd become involved in. He was great at everything, and almost everyone seemed to adore him.

While Addison was enjoying his new life at the yoga center and the college, Jeremy had finished up his junior year at Gilroy High. His grades were average—generally C's, but he was fine with that. He decided to get a job over the summer. Money—or the lack thereof—had become an issue for him. He found a job at a local automotive store. The one thing he excelled at was taking care of automobiles. Jeremy knew everything about cars. He loved them. Becoming a race-car driver was his dream. It always had been, since his early years of playing with cars in the sandbox with his mom.

Jeremy had often wished he could be more like his dad and invent cool things, but that was not to be, and he knew it. Addison had the brains and could relate better to their dad. Addy understood Bob's scientific way of looking at life. Jeremy knew he couldn't compete with that. He also knew his dad loved him just the way he was. But still . . . Jeremy sat at the kitchen table, stewing over the thought of how well Addison and Bob got on together. They spoke the same language, that of intellectuals. This was not within Jeremy's realm. He was saddened. *I think Addison fills something in Dad that I can't. I'll never be that smart. I can't look at a scientific journal and talk and laugh about ideas with Dad like Addison does. I'm not as good as he is, no matter what everyone says. I'm just an average teenage guy. I'm not an intellectual. Dad will never look at me the way he does at Addison. He's perfect! I'm nowhere near perfect! How can I compete with that? I can't!*

Just then Bob entered the kitchen, looking for an ice-cold glass of water before he headed back down into the cellar. He filled his glass and joined his son at the table for a moment. This brightened Jeremy's mood. "Dad, guess what? I got a job at Pete's Auto Parts for the summer," Jeremy said with some pride. "It only pays minimum wage, but I get to work with car stuff."

"That's great, son," replied his father. "I think that's super."

"I'm good with cars, Dad, and I love them. I think it's a great first job for me, I really do."

"Then that's what you should do, Jeremy. Do what you love," Bob told him. "You only get one chance at this life, right?"

"That's what they say, Dad."

"'They gotta be right!" Father and son laughed.

"But I'm no Addison, Dad," Jeremy explained with some seriousness. "I am who I am. I don't know science, but I do know cars."

"I know you're not, Jeremy. I don't want two Addisons. You know who you are, and you are following your dreams. I admire you for that." Bob leaned over and tousled Jeremy's hair. "You know, I think you're the cool one of the two of you. You've got it going on! I was never cool or good with cars. That's all a mystery to me. I just don't get cars much at all. But I do admire your knowledge of them."

"Thanks, Dad. That means a lot. But I think you and Addy are cool too. Just not about car stuff. We're just different that way, right?"

"Yep. You got that right! You're on the right track, Jeremy. Good luck on your new job!" Then Bob finished his glass of water, got up from his chair, and went back down to the cellar to continue his work on the cyborg plans. Jeremy went off to his room and fired up his computer. *Dad doesn't want two Addisons,* Jeremy thought to himself. *That's good, because I'll never be anything like him!*

Jeremy's thoughts were interrupted by the jarring sound of his ringing cell phone. It was Al. "Dude—wanna go to the Hover-Car Rink? I have a need for speed! You in?"

"Are you kidding? Of course! How about tomorrow, around one? I'll come and get you."

"Sounds great! See you then." Al hung up. *Lovin' this!* He began rubbing his hands together. It had been a few weeks since he and Jeremy had hit the rink, and he was having withdrawal symptoms. *I need some excitement in my life,* Al thought as he turned on the TV and plopped down on his couch. *Gotta go fast—gotta move!*

The mere thought of racing made Jeremy's adrenalin rush through his body. This type of racing was a brand-new phenomenon that was sweeping the country. Hover-car racing involved igniting four jet engines underneath the vehicle, which pushed it up above the ground. When the race began, the wheels folded underneath the car, the jet engines at the ready, and the car, at the bidding of the driver, rose up a foot or so above the ground and took off at speeds of over 150 mph.

Hover cars had been used for years by the military but were now being sold to the public. The racing community embraced the new vehicles, and thus Hover-Car Racing was born. The cars at the specially designed rinks were outfitted with bumpers to make them extra safe for any and all passengers. Their safety record was unsurpassed. In fact, hover-car racing was safer than driving a car to the mall and back. Parents had to sign a release form so their kids could participate in the racing events. The rink in San Martin had a perfect safety record, so Jeremy's and Al's parents couldn't say no.

The San Martin Hover-Car Racing Rink was only a few miles away from Jeremy's and Al's homes. It was located next to the local airport. Many of the high-tech execs in the area would fly their clients via corporate jets there for an afternoon of racing fun. Al and Jeremy went as often as they could. The track allowed for twenty cars to race at a time. Everyone was required to use helmets. The course was circular and was built in a bowl shape, allowing the cars to hover at a 90-degree angle, if they so chose. The cars' bumpers were designed so that drivers could hit each other in a friendly sort of way. However, 180-degree hits were strictly prohibited. They were dangerous, and a number of drivers had lost their lives when hit that way. A 180-degree hit occurred when a driver would drive on the rim of the track and hit the car next to him hard, causing the other car to be thrown upside down and perhaps injuring the driver—or worse. If someone made a hard hit like that, he would lose his racing privilege, or possibly go to jail.

The sport was highly addictive. And it was a whole lot of fun. The next day Jeremy and Al found themselves at the rink, choosing their respective cars for an afternoon race. The stadium was filled with onlookers that mild, sunny day. "I like this one," Jeremy said, eyeing a red Mustang fastback.

"Of course you do," Al replied. "It looks just like your 'stang.'"

"Well, this is the one I'm gonna drive. What about you?"

"This one." Al had already climbed into a bright-yellow sports car. "It suits me, don't you think?"

"It was made for you, Al, I swear."

They drove to the starting line. Shortly thereafter, a short man with a checkered flag arrived. He grabbed the mike. "Gentlemen and ladies, please start your engines."

The racers all pressed their starters. The cars whirred and rose up a foot into the air. "On your mark . . . Get set . . . *Go!*" The checkered flag was drawn down, and about twenty cars took off, moving around the track at breakneck speed. Al was screaming "Yee-haw!" while Jeremy was intense, focused on the race.

The cars made five laps, and over the course of that time, Jeremy and Al found themselves neck and neck with a sporty black car that was in the lead. They had one lap to go. Jeremy went up the side of the track and peered into the car to see who was driving. It was a girl, someone he knew from school, but he didn't know her name. He tapped his car against hers and her car wavered a bit. It righted itself pretty quickly. The girl looked over and obviously recognized Jeremy. She smiled at him. He smiled back. She slammed her car into his, which forced him to hit his brakes. In the meantime, Al had whizzed by both of them, easily winning the race.

"That was awesome," Al said as they all emerged from their cars. "Great race!"

"Yeah, congratulations, Al!" Jeremy said. "I'm glad you won, if I couldn't!" He smiled. "I kinda got caught up trying to get ahead of her." He pointed to the girl exiting her car.

"I noticed!" Al replied, laughing. "I oughta thank her!"

CHAPTER 7

— ■ —

IS IT LOVE?

N ot only had Addy created a pretty great life for himself in record time, he and Alexandra had also become an item. Alexandra and Addison were seen together a lot around town. Addison enjoyed bowling, as did Alex, so they spent a good deal of time over the summer at the local bowling alley. Addison, not surprisingly, had a near-perfect bowling style, one that went along with his near-perfect bowling score. This, however, did not bother or frustrate Alex. She, along with most of the other girls and women who came across Addison's path, found him to be both good-looking and charming. The fact that he was heads above everyone in everything he undertook did not deter any woman from spending as much time as possible with him.

"Can I get you anything from the restaurant, Alex?" asked Addison as they were about to start another game.

"Maybe a Coke, Addy. Thanks."

"Done." Addison went to the alley restaurant for the drink, and Alex sat in the bowling pit by their lane, thinking about Addison.

He is such a great guy, Alex thought. *And very smart and nice. But I'm not sure I want to get involved with a cyborg—or is something else bothering me?* She wasn't sure how she felt about Addison, except that she was not exactly drawn to him romantically. She couldn't, however, put her finger on exactly why that was. He had everything. He was smart, gorgeous, nice, and respectful of women. But still something was missing. But what exactly that was, she didn't know.

In the meantime, Al had gone over to Jeremy's house. "Hey, dude."

"Hey. Want some ice cream? I'm starving."

"You bet."

"So, what's been going on with you lately?" Al followed Jeremy into the kitchen for the ice cream.

"I've just been hanging around—working, you know, just doing stuff," Jeremy responded. He served them some carob ice cream, and then they sat down at the kitchen table.

"So, my sister and your brother," Al mused. "Who woulda thunk it . . ." He shook his head.

"I would've," Jeremy replied sullenly. "He's got it all. Brains, looks, talent . . ."

"Yeah, but he's not you, dude. You're a great guy. And I know you like her. Why don't you ask her out?"

"Because she's dating Addison," Jeremy replied, putting a spoonful of the carob splendor into his mouth. "It wouldn't be cool. He's my, um, brother, I guess. It's against the code, dude. And Addison and I don't exactly gel as it is. I mean, he's okay, but I'm not so wild about him, like everyone else seems to be."

"Me neither," Al agreed. "For one thing, he's dating my sister. And for another thing, he's a cyborg. That's just not right, you know?" Al was staring at Jeremy intently. "What if they get married? Could they even have kids? And what kind of kids would they be? I don't know . . ."

Just then, they heard Jeremy's dad coming up the cellar stairs. "Hi, Dad," Jeremy said as his dad entered the kitchen.

"Hi, guys," Bob replied. "Al, I couldn't help overhear your concerns about Addison. I think you guys are getting way ahead of yourselves. Addison and Alexandra are just dating, you know? They don't know each other well enough yet to even consider marriage."

"What about romance, Dr. Bob?" Al asked.

Bob took a seat at the table. "I guess there will be romance in his life; in fact, I hope there is. I'd hate to think of him all alone for eternity."

"But he's a cyborg, Mr. Taylor, not a real guy," Al replied.

"He *is* a real guy, Al," Bob responded. "He's not just a machine. Please don't think of him that way."

Al looked uncomfortable. "Look, Mr. Taylor, the guy's dating my sister. I guess I'd be suspicious of anyone dating her. But *him*? I gotta protect her, you know."

"That's understandable, Al. I got you. But you don't have to worry about Addy. You have my word."

"Dad," Jeremy asked, changing the subject. "What're you doing down in the cellar? I thought you'd be spending more time up here now that you're finished working on Addison."

"I plan to, Jeremy. I'm just finishing up putting together all of the plans and patents for Vladimir on Addison. Once that's complete and I hand everything over to him per our agreement, I won't be down there as much anymore. I plan to spend more time with my number-one son." Bob gave Jeremy a hug. "We'll do a lot more things together, I promise."

"I'm looking forward to that, Dad," Jeremy replied, hugging Bob back. "I can't wait."

"Me too, son. Just give me a little more time. Then you'll be spending so much time with me you'll probably get sick of me!" With that, Bob gave his son a kiss on the head and turned around, heading back to the cellar.

Just a little while longer, Bob thought as he sat back down at his desk downstairs. *I gotta make sure I have everything together for Vladimir, and then I'll be free—free to do whatever I want, and I won't have to worry about anything anymore. Not Jeremy being alone, not money—not anything.* Bob turned his computer back on and began combining files again, meticulously cataloging all his entries. He was very thorough, always had been. He had often thought his tendency toward perfection in his work was more of a curse than a blessing.

CHAPTER 8

---------- ▪ ----------

WORK AND CASEY

It was a bright, sunny Saturday morning, and Jeremy was scheduled to work at Pete's most of the day. His boss, Pete, was a second-generation Chinese-American. He had a beautiful daughter, Casey, who was going to be a senior in high school in the fall, like Jeremy. They attended the same school and knew of each other, though they hadn't been friends. Casey had been in several of Jeremy's classes over the course of the last few years. They were friendly to one another, but that was as far as it went. They were both scheduled to work that Saturday.

"Hi, Casey," Jeremy greeted his classmate with a smile as he entered the automotive store for his first day at work.

"Hi, Jeremy. My dad says you're working here now over the summer. That's great. It'll give me a bit of a break," she responded, throwing her long black hair behind her shoulders. "Dad said that once you get the hang of things around here I can take off a bit."

"Glad I can help!" Jeremy said with a laugh. *She's very pretty*, he thought. Casey was a few inches shorter than he was, probably about five foot four, he figured. She had pretty, almond-shaped, dark-brown eyes, and she parted her hair on the side, so that it fell slightly over one eye, causing her to pull it back behind her ear when she was looking down. Just then, something dawned on him.

"Casey?"

"Yes?"

"Was that you at the racetrack last week? The girl in the black car?"

"Um . . . why yes, it was. You remembered!"

"Of course I remembered. That was some great driving you did."

"Thanks!" Casey said and she smiled.

They had a half hour until the store opened. Casey gave Jeremy the tour of the store so that he knew where everything was. Then, she showed him how to use the register. He felt he had it all together—until the store opened and it got busy. "Where's the windshield wipers for a 2020 Honda Accord?" asked a customer. Jeremy wasn't sure. He asked Casey, who showed the customer how to find what he was looking for in a book at the back of the store.

"Thanks, Casey. I didn't know—"

"It's your first day, Jeremy. It'll take you a while to get the hang of things. Don't worry about it." Casey ran off to help another customer, leaving Jeremy, who was feeling useless and flustered.

"Jeremy, can you help a customer in aisle 5?" Casey asked, while simultaneously ringing someone up in the front. Jeremy went to aisle 5. The customer was looking for some touch-up paint for a 2025 Prius. Again Jeremy couldn't help.

"Casey," Jeremy said raising his voice, "please give me a hand in aisle 5 when you get a chance." He smiled uneasily at the customer. "She'll be here in a minute," he said, straightening some oil cans on a shelf nearby in order to look busy. Jeremy's day went pretty much that way from nine o'clock till five o'clock. When the store closed, he was exhausted and relieved. "Wow, there's a lot to know around here," he exclaimed.

"Yeah, there's a lot to learn," Casey agreed. "But you'll get the hang of it soon enough, I promise," she said as she closed out the register. "So, anyway, Dad is on tomorrow. You'll be working with him then. We open at ten on Sundays. You get to sleep in!"

"I'll definitely be taking advantage of that, Casey. And by the way, I want you to know that you're a great teacher," Jeremy said. He meant every word. "I couldn't have survived without you."

"Thanks, Jeremy. I'm looking forward to working with you." They walked out to where their cars were parked behind the store. Casey had a Mustang convertible too, only hers was white.

"Love your choice in cars, Casey," Jeremy joked while jumping into his car.

"You've got good taste yourself," Casey shot back. "I'll see you Monday."

"See you then."

As Jeremy left the parking lot and pointed his car toward home, he started thinking about the day he'd just had. It hadn't been so bad. Casey had been helpful and friendly to him. *I think I'm going to like working at Pete's*, he thought. *And Casey's kinda cute.* He sped off down the road, smiling to himself.

CHAPTER 9

GARLIC FESTIVAL FUN

"Dude, the Gilroy Garlic Festival is coming up. Wanna go?" asked Al as he looked through the newspaper strewn across Jeremy's kitchen table. Jeremy had always enjoyed the festival. He and his dad and mom had gone every year when he was growing up. In the last several years, he and Al had gone together, joining other friends to peruse the fabulous and interesting foodstuffs. They always finished the day with a bowl of garlic ice cream. "Sure, Al, I'm in. I just have to check my hours for next weekend."

"Great! Alex is going with Addison. But she says that Addison is not a fan of garlic. Wonder how he'll feel about it when we get him some of that awesome garlic ice cream?"

"Dude, let's not tell him what's in it!"

"Yeah! It'll be great to see his face!" Jeremy smiled. It was a rare treat to see Addison not being perfect. It was worth going to the festival just for that. But he always enjoyed the event—the country music, the booths with lots of interesting arts and crafts, the great food, and the whole feel of the fair. He especially loved the garlic fries. He and his mom and dad had always enjoyed the overall experience. *Great memories*, he thought as he fixed a snack for himself and Al.

"How's work?" Al wanted to know. "You like it at Pete's?"

"Casey works there. Remember her? She's kinda nice."

"Really? You mean that pretty Asian chick?"

"Yeah. She taught me the register and showed me around the store. She's a great teacher. I was really floundering around there in the beginning. She was super calm and didn't make me feel like a fool or anything for not knowing things. I'm going to enjoy working with her."

"Hmm. Jeremy, do you like her? I mean, would you date her?" Al wanted to know. "Maybe you should invite her to the Garlic Festival. I was thinking of asking Louisa from gym class. She's always been nice to me."

"Al, you are brilliant, my man," Jeremy said with a smile as he took a bite of his peanut butter and jam. "Sounds like a plan."

The following Sunday, Jeremy and Al met up with Casey, Louisa, Alex, and Addison at the entrance of the Gilroy Garlic Festival. It was a typical hot and sunny summer day. The air was filled with the smell of garlic coming from the dozens of food booths at the fair, all of whom were espousing their version of gourmet garlic foodstuffs. Garlic was part of the lifeblood of the town. It was grown there in abundance and pressed there, as well. Living in Gilroy, the friends had long since embraced the smell of "the stinking rose." Addison, however, was obviously grossed out by the strong aroma. "Wow, the smell is powerful," he noted. "You all *like* this?" He looked incredulous.

"Of course we like it," Alex responded. "We are Gilroyans. Gilroyans love garlic. That's just the way it is!"

"Okay, Alex. I get that you love Gilroy. But does that necessarily mean you have to love *garlic*?" Addison asked haltingly. "I mean, I don't."

"Well, dude, don't say that too loud. Some of the old timers here might hear you, and then you'll have some explaining to do." Al laughed.

"Yeah," Jeremy chimed in. "The oldies here in town don't take too kindly to people who hate garlic."

"I'll take my chances," responded Addison.

The day literally flew by. Everyone had a great time at the festival, even Addison, who at least was fond of country music. That endeared him to the group. At the end of the day, they all stopped at the garlic ice cream stand. Jeremy bought some for everyone. Addison was holding a table under a tent for them to sit at and enjoy their last treat of the day. He didn't know that the ice cream had garlic in it. Everyone waited for him to take a bite. It was well known that Addison was having his first serving of the pungent-tasting dessert and that he was blissfully unaware of what he was about to ingest.

"Hey, you guys, this is good ice cream," Addison said, licking his lips. He was in the middle of his second bite when the garlic hit him. His throat started to swell. The garlic moved up his esophagus, into his mouth. He turned a shade of red Jeremy hadn't seen on him before. "What the heck is this?" he said disbelievingly. "There's something in this . . . *garlic!*"

Everyone started laughing, obviously enjoying their little prank on Addison. Jeremy pulled out his phone and took a picture of Addy, his face red and twisted in disgust. Al and Alex simultaneously took out their phones and took shots as well. "It's garlic ice cream," Alex said, giving Addison a hug. "Sorry, hon. We all wanted to surprise you."

"Yeah, well you did that!" Addison said, and he laughed.

"It's something everyone tries who comes here—at least one time," chimed in Casey. "For me, once was enough!"

"For you *and* me!" retorted Addison. "Um, I think I've had enough, guys. I'm ready to go."

It was early evening as they all walked to the festival exit and said good-bye to one another. "Another successful Garlic Festival, eh, Al?" Jeremy asked while they walked to his car.

"The best yet, Jeremy. Addison was a pretty good sport, considering, didn't you think?"

"Yeah, I guess bro's not so bad. As far as I'm concerned, he can't be perfect if he doesn't love garlic."

"You can say that again."

They jumped into Jeremy's car and sped home. "I gotta tell Dad that he missed a great festival," Jeremy added. "You know, he loves Gilroy garlic more than anyone I know."

"What's he up to these days?"

"Still putting together all of the documents for Human-istic on the cyborg thing. Dad's like one of those scientists that's very detail-oriented, but he's got papers everywhere—all over downstairs in the cellar. It'll take him weeks to pull everything together," Jeremy said as he turned into his driveway.

"It'll be so worth it when he's done, dude. You guys'll be rich!" Al got out of the car. "See ya," he said, waving good-bye.

"See ya." Jeremy parked his car in the driveway and entered his house. He felt exhausted. He heard his dad downstairs.

"Hi, Jeremy!" his dad yelled from the cellar. "Did you have a good time?"

"Yes, Dad!" Jeremy yelled back. "I'll tell you about it later! I'm gonna go hang out in my room!"

"Later, Jeremy!"

Jeremy was lying on his bed playing Sudoku on his iPhone when Addison entered the room. "Hi, Jeremy," he said, hanging up his jacket and sitting down on his bed. "I had a great time tonight."

"Me too; it was a lot of fun," Jeremy agreed. "We'll have to do more double dating. Casey's okay, don't you think?"

"I thought she was cool. She's pretty too."

Just then Bob came up the stairs and knocked on the boys' door. "Can I come in?" he asked.

"Come in!" the boys answered.

"So, how was the Garlic Festival? Sorry I missed it. At least I got a lot of work done."

"It was fun, Dad, really. But we missed you." Jeremy was sincere.

"Dad, they played me—gave me a bunch of that garlic ice cream without telling me! Yuck! I thought I was going to hurl!" Addison made a face.

Jeremy and Bob were both amused.

"Well, son, guess you've been baptized into the Gilroy garlic family. Once you've tasted that ice cream, you'll never be the same again! I predict that one day you will love garlic as much as I do, and that's saying something."

Addy shook his head. "If that day comes, Dad, I'll know that life as we've known it has ended."

They all talked awhile about the events of the day, and then Bob left so the boys could get ready for bed. As Jeremy turned out the light and lay down, he realized that he had actually enjoyed having Addison around that day. He had been fun to be with and had gotten along great with everyone. For the first time, he was happy that his father had created him and that Addison was a part of the family.

The next morning, Jeremy heard the phone ring. He ran to pick it up, and it was Al. "Dude, I have to tell you something, but I'm not supposed to . . ."

"Does it have to do with me?" asked Jeremy, intrigued.

"Yeah. Okay, it's Alex. She's jealous of Casey." Al laughed. "She was pissed that you were dating her."

"I don't get it, Al. She's never shown any interest in me."

"Yeah, but she doesn't want anyone *else* to have you!" Al said enthusiastically. "I think she knew you liked her," Al continued, "and now she feels like you are kinda cheating on her. *Women!* My sister makes no sense to me," he finished.

"Does she still like Addison?" Jeremy asked.

"I think so, but she complains that he's not very romantic."

"Wow," Jeremy responded. "If Mr. Perfect isn't perfect enough for her, what hope do I have with her—or for that matter, what hope do any of us guys have with *any* girl?"

"Maybe they don't want perfect but want to fix us imperfect slobs up, you know? Girls like to fix people," Al finished.

"Al, sometimes you are so profound," Jeremy said with a laugh.

"Yeah, I'm so smart," Al said sarcastically. "Well, just thought you'd like to know. Don't tell Alex I told you, though."

"Your secret's safe with me!" Jeremy hung up. *Girls*, he thought, walking out of his house to his car. "Well, Casey's great. I enjoy being with her. And I understand her better than Alex. The timing never seems right for Alex and me."

Jeremy drove to work, mulling over his feelings about the girls in his life and things in general. For the first time in a while he felt that everything was going pretty well and was under control. Life was indeed going very well for Jeremy Taylor.

CHAPTER 10

·

NO, NOT THAT

A few weeks later, Bob was home alone on a stormy, hot Saturday afternoon. He was working in his cellar as usual. Jeremy was at work; Essie and Addison were giving their yoga classes downtown, and Bob had finally put the finishing touches on the files describing the plans for his cyborg development for Human-istic—the plans that would make him and Rob millionaires—maybe billionaires—in short order.

Bob sat back in his old swivel chair and smiled. He could finally give his family the stability and financial security he'd always wanted to. Once Human-istic started manufacturing and selling these cyborgs, he reasoned, not only would they be helpful to society but he would be getting a hefty royalty for every one sold. In his mind he began waxing poetic. It bothered him a bit—mass producing a creation that was so close to being human. But it would not be a creation of God, just man, he reasoned. The cyborgs had no soul, no real link whatsoever to what the Grand Master had created. Bottom line: they were only to be Human-istic robots with some human DNA thrown in, nothing more. Not really . . .

Besides putting together the plans for the cyborgs, Bob had also been working on something new. It was something mankind would definitely embrace, should he find a breakthrough. His cellar was filled with all kinds of vials and test tubes filled with bubbling, colorful concoctions that were being heated at varying degrees to see if, when heated, they might give him a winning potion of sorts. He hoped one of these concoctions would someday defeat a nemesis of his—cancer. Cancer had robbed him of his beautiful wife, Suzanne. Cancer had robbed him of a happy, peaceful, fulfilling, and loving family life that included the woman of his dreams. *Someday*, Bob thought, sighing, *I will find a cure for this horrible disease.*

Just then the phone rang. He picked up his old-fashioned phone. (Jeremy was always after him to just use his cell phone, but Bob said the old plug-in phone had sentimental value. He'd used it for a quarter of a century and wasn't about to give it up now.) It was Rob on the other end.

"Hey, buddy, how are things going?" Rob asked. He was sitting in front of his television with some chips. He'd been enjoying a baseball game that was dragging on a bit.

"I'll tell you, my friend. Things are going very well, very well indeed."

"You get a date or something?" Rob said, grinning.

Bob laughed. "No, nothing that interesting. However, I've finally finished the plans for the cyborg production. We're gonna be rich, Rob."

All of a sudden, a loud crack of thunder shook Bob. "Wow, that was loud. Maybe we should—"

Both Rob and Bob heard another loud crack of thunder. This time, however, lightning had hit the telephone line and traveled down into Bob's receiver. The powerful blast threw him across the room and knocked over some of the glassware and the Bunsen burner that had been heating the liquid from underneath. Bob had hit his head against the wall, and he was unconscious.

"Bob, can you hear me? Bob!" Rob was panicking. He'd heard a loud noise. Then the phone line had gone dead. He ran out of his house to his car and sped off in the direction of Bob's house. Rob was really scared.

Al saw the fire from his bedroom. The flames were billowing up into the dark, rainy sky. "Oh my God! Jeremy's house is on fire!" Al picked up the phone and called 911. He then put in a call to Jeremy at work. "Dude, your house is on fire—you better get over here!" Al exclaimed, running outside. Just then he saw something come out of the house. He sprinted over to the Taylor's home in time to see Botty descending the front steps and coming toward him.

"I called to Mr. Taylor," Botty said. "He was down in the basement, where the fire started. It was a lightning strike. He did not answer me. I tried to go down and get him, but the fire was too much. I was unable to do so. I came for help. Can you help me save Mr. Taylor, Al?"

Al was visibly upset by this time, tears coming fast and furious. "Botty, we can't . . . we can't save him now," Al replied, hugging the robot for support. "No one can go in that house now and survive." Just then he saw something else emerge slowly from the home. "Sammy!" Al called, recognizing the dog. "Here, Sammy! Here, boy!" The dog, hearing his name being called, dutifully came trotting up to Al, who bent down, scooping the dog in his arms. "You're a miracle, you know that?" Al kissed the dog. Sammy wagged his tail weakly. The smoke had made him groggy. His fur was somewhat singed and smelled acrid.

Jeremy had sped home to find Essie and Addison already there, staring at the house in disbelief. The firemen were also there—working hard with their fire hoses, ladders, and crew to put the fire out, but the fierce flames had already engulfed the house.

Al, spying Jeremy, walked over to meet his friend, Botty right behind him. "It started in the basement," he cried, hugging Jeremy, and then he continued, "That fireman over there—he's the one in charge." He pointed to a large man who was on a radio, watching the scene from one of the fire engines.

Jeremy ran over to the fire chief, with the others following. "I—I think my dad's in there!" he screamed, tears streaming down his face.

"I'm sorry . . . your name is?" the chief responded, focused on the goings-on at the scene.

"Jeremy."

"Well, Jeremy we haven't been able to get inside the home yet to look for anyone. I'll let the guys know to look out for your dad." He radioed the information to the firemen working on the house exterior.

The flames had consumed most of the house by the time Rob arrived on the scene. He was visibly shaken by what he saw. He threw his car in park and ran over to where Essie, Jeremy, Al, Botty, and Addison were standing.

"I was just talking to Bob on the phone, Essie," Rob exclaimed, his eyes on the fire in disbelief. "He was downstairs in the cellar. He'd just finished the plans for Vladimir . . ." Rob trailed off.

Essie ran quickly over to the fireman in charge. "My brother's in the basement, the basement!" she yelled. The firefighter sat her down on the curb. "I am sorry, miss. That part of the house has already been completely destroyed. No one could've survived in that part of your home . . ." Essie looked deeply into his soft, sad-looking brown eyes. She understood. Her brother was gone. The chief held her close as she wept softly into his chest. "He was my only brother," she said quietly through her tears. "My nephew doesn't have a mother or a father anymore."

"Aunt Essie?" Jeremy came to her side. He kneeled down and looked her in the eyes. "Dad . . . he's gone, isn't he?" Jeremy asked, not really wanting to hear the answer.

"Yes, dear, he is," Essie replied softly. "We'll get by somehow—don't you worry." Essie looked both sad and distressed. She really had no idea what they would do now.

Al, Addison, and Rob overheard the conversation. "Essie?" Rob took both her hands in his. "I'd love it if you, Jeremy, and Addison would move in with me. Botty and Sammy too. Hell, I have that big house with no one to share it with. I consider you guys to be my family anyway. Please come." Rob was in earnest. He loved all of the Taylors. "Please . . ." He looked beseechingly at Jeremy and Addison. "Boys, would you like to move in with me? Please say you will."

"Rob, thank you for the offer . . ." Jeremy gave him a hug.

"I'd move in if Essie will come too," Addison added, looking to Essie to make the final decision.

"Thank you, Rob. I don't know what we'd do without you," Essie said, standing up. "Yes, we will move in with you. I really appreciate what you're doing for us, Rob."

Later, Al went home to fill his family in on the Taylor's loss. Alex and Al, along with their mom and dad, came over and did what they could to show their support. After they'd gone home, the Taylors and Rob stayed a while longer, surveying what was left of the Taylor's residence. The house was completely destroyed. Some of the furnishings had survived, nothing more. It was, for all intents and purposes, a total loss.

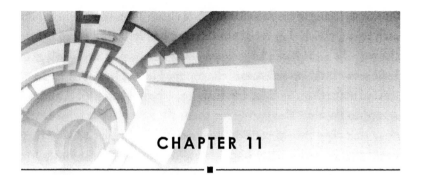

CHAPTER 11

──────────────■──────────────

FROM THE ASHES

The next few days were a blur for Jeremy and his family. The police had called because the firemen had found Jeremy's dad's remains in the cellar and had matched his teeth to dental records, so there was no doubt whose body had been found. It was no surprise to Jeremy or anyone else. Rob and Essie planned the funeral for the following Friday. Bob had always wanted to be cremated, so there wasn't much to do to prepare for that. Then there was the need to go back to the house and try and retrieve anything of value that hadn't been destroyed in the fire. Jeremy and Addison found some clothes that hadn't been ruined, and the upstairs bedroom furniture, though smoke damaged, had not been destroyed. Essie decided to put all the furniture and other belongings that were salvageable in a storage unit at the edge of town. They'd deal with their things later; now it was time for Essie to honor her brother's memory and get herself and the boys situated and comfortable at Rob's house.

Rob's home was beautiful, with lots of room for everyone to live comfortably together. There was a large family room with picture windows facing out over the southern Santa Clara Valley. Rob had acres of land, with lots of trees surrounding his home. The furnishings were modern and typical of a man who'd been a lifelong bachelor: stark black-and-glass tables, with black leather sofas and chairs in a semicircle facing toward the Santa Clara views. The boys each had their own room, which they loved after having had to share a room before the tragedy. Essie had a large bedroom of her own as well. Rob gave Essie some funds to redecorate the rooms. He said he hadn't had any time to make them look decent. Essie knew he was being kind, and she agreed to do some decorating for them all. Rob made it abundantly clear that they should consider his house their home and that they could stay as long as they liked. He told them he lived a lonely life and that they were actually doing him a favor by moving in. Everyone appreciated Rob's generosity and genuine friendship.

The funeral was held at the local Presbyterian Church and was filled with friends and associates of Bob's from Human-istic. Alex was one of the first of Jeremy's friends to arrive. She was visibly upset about Bob's untimely death. "You know I loved your dad, right, Jeremy?" she asked, tears streaming down her face. Jeremy let her know that he knew they'd had a special bond. Alex had spent a great deal of time with his dad in the cellar, working on his various scientific projects with him. Alex and Bob had similar interests in science—and those interests had never been shared by Jeremy. Not for Jeremy's lack of trying to get into science, but it just wasn't a passion of his, no matter how hard he had tried. Alex and his dad were kindred spirits around their interest in science. It had brought them together time and time again. The only scientific project they hadn't shared was Bob's work on the creation of Addison.

After the guests had been greeted at the church, everyone took a seat for the ceremony. The family's minister, Pastor John, opened the service with a prayer and a short sermon, and then he asked whether anyone would like to say a few words about Bob Taylor. Essie spoke first, and then Rob took a turn. Their stories about their relationships to Bob were lovely and heartfelt. When Jeremy stood up to speak, there wasn't a dry eye in the house. As Jeremy began his speech, Addison got up and started for the exit. He couldn't take the raw pain and emotion that was being expressed by his new friends and family.

Addison walked through the back doors to the narthex, where the guests had entered the church just a while before. As he stood there, he noticed a tall man, who had seemed to just appear, reading the church bulletin about Bob Taylor. Addison looked over at him, then away, and then he did a double take. The man who had turned to face Addison was Bob himself—looking very much alive, well, and happy.

"Dad!"

"Shh, son," Bob said with a smile. "I just wanted to see who would show up at my funeral." Bob grinned.

"Dad, aren't you . . ." Addison looked at him in disbelief. "Dead?"

"Yeah, I'm dead, but as you can see, I am okay. I wanted you kids to know that I'm all right, and so is Suzanne. It's been great seeing her again." Bob smiled wider. "Tell Jeremy his mom and dad are fine. That we're all right. And Addy? We love you. You are a wonderful young man. Keep Jeremy on an even keel for me, will you?"

"Sure, Dad . . ." Addison was not really certain about what he was seeing and hearing. Just as quickly as he'd come, Bob disappeared again. Addison was in shock; he stood there in disbelief, not moving, for a good fifteen minutes. When he had composed himself, Addison went back into the church and sat next to Jeremy, who had just finished his homage to his father.

Jeremy looked at his brother, who was looking kind of pale. "You okay, Addy? You look pretty weird."

"Yeah, I am okay, I guess. I'll tell you about it later," Addison whispered back.

After the ceremony the guests were invited to Rob's home for some food and drink, to celebrate Bob's life. Vladimir, who had made a beautiful statement at the funeral about Bob and all that he had done to help build the company, came up to Rob shortly after arriving at his home. "I'm so sorry about Bob," Vladimir began. "Such a tragedy, no question. This may not be the best time to bring this up Rob, but I was wondering—do you have the project files for the cyborg Bob was working on? We need to get a move on the production of 'em," he said, pointing his drink in the direction of Addison.

"Vladimir," Rob said, in distress, "this is *not* the time or the place—"

"Please, Rob, don't give me that. You are just as passionate about making those things as I am."

"Maybe so, Vladimir, but can we talk about it Monday at work?"

"Yeah, that'll be fine. But first thing. I want to see you in my office at 9:00 a.m. sharp!" Vladimir walked off and met up with his wife, who was talking with Essie. "Your brother was a genius you know," Vladimir interjected.

"My brother was smart," Essie concurred. "But he was an even better brother and father."

"Nice to hear," Vladimir added. Then, changing the subject, he moved closer to his wife and interjected, "Janice, it's time to go." He grabbed her drink and put it down on the table. "Bye, Essie," he said as Janice waved her hand in her general direction. Janice allowed her husband to guide her outside to their car, and they drove away.

Rob, who'd seen the entire interaction, went to Essie's side. "Vladimir wants the cyborg plans," he reported to Essie. "And he wants them now. I have to meet with him about them first thing Monday morning."

"Do you have the plans, Rob?" Essie asked, looking concerned.

"No. Bob told me he had just finished them," he said sadly. "They're probably lost forever. I'm assuming they were destroyed in the fire. Nothing was salvaged from the cellar."

"Well, we'll have a look this weekend . . . maybe we can find them," Essie said with a sigh. "You don't have anything you can give to Vladimir on Monday regarding the plans?"

"I've got my part of the work on my computer," Bob replied, "but not a thing on Bob's work." They looked at each other, knowing that the money they'd been hoping for from the sales of the cyborgs might not materialize without Bob's work being found. "We'll discuss it tomorrow," Rob said, giving Essie a hug. "Don't worry. We'll be all right, with or without that money."

CHAPTER 12

———————————————— ■ ————————————————

SEEING IS BELIEVING

Saturday was a day of rest for the Taylors. The stress of losing Bob and their home was taking its toll. Essie made breakfast for everyone, and they all sat in silence for a while. Finally, Addison spoke. "Guys? I have something weird to tell you . . ."

"What is it, Addy?" Essie asked, placing her glass of orange juice down on the table.

"Well . . . yesterday, during the funeral, I went out to the front of the church and I saw . . . well . . . I saw Dad."

"What?" Jeremy looked at his brother as if he were crazy.

"I know, it sounds kinda nutty, but when you were speaking at the funeral, Jeremy, Dad appeared to me—he was just standing there in the front of the church. He wanted you to know he was okay. He said your mom is okay too. He really looked fine—great, actually."

"Are you sure you weren't really having a nervous breakdown, bro?" Jeremy wanted to know. He eyed his brother suspiciously.

"Jeremy, it was *him*, I swear!" Addison knew how it sounded.

"I believe you," Essie said, putting her glass of orange juice down and looking very serious. She focused her energy on her nephew. "Jeremy, I believe with all my heart that we do live on after death. We just move onto a different plane of existence, you know? I think we probably live on another level that vibrates higher than this one, which is why it's often hard to see those who've gone to the other side. It'd take a lot of energy for the spirits to lower their vibration to be seen by us. At least, that's what I hear!"

"You *really* believe that, Essie?" Rob asked while buttering his bread. To say he was skeptical was a huge understatement.

"Yes, Rob, I really do. My brother just visited us from beyond the grave, for gosh sakes! You heard Addy. He *saw* him. He *spoke* to him! Addy doesn't lie. What more proof do you need?"

"Well, if I'd seen him and talked to him, then I'd believe."

"Well, Rob, next time he comes here to visit, we'll just ask him to stop by and say hello to you, right boys?"

"Sure," Jeremy replied, amused. To tell the truth, he was a little skeptical himself, but he wasn't about to say anything in that regard to Aunt Essie.

"Right!" Addison agreed.

"Great. It's settled." Essie ate her eggs in angry silence, feeling justified in her stance on the subject but upset that Rob didn't believe her. Maybe he thought she was a little loony because of her beliefs. She wasn't sure.

"Hey, guys," Rob began, wanting desperately to change the subject. "Can you come with me to your house to look for CDs or papers or something with the cyborg plans on them? Vladimir is bugging me to give him that info as soon as possible. In fact, he's set up a meeting Monday morning with me to discuss the plans. We've gotta find something I can give him!" Rob was obviously getting nervous about the meeting with his boss.

"No problem," Jeremy offered. "I can help."

"Yeah, I can help too," Addison replied.

"Would you like me to come too?" Botty asked while continuing to clear the table.

"No, Botty. You stay here and help Aunt Essie. We've got this under control, right boys?"

Jeremy and Addison nodded in the affirmative.

After the breakfast dishes were done, the guys set off for what was left of the Taylor's house. When they arrived, they were taken aback. The whole structure had collapsed. There were chunks of partly burned, wet two-by-fours strewn all over the property. Piles and piles of wood, mixed with parts of furniture and bits of rug and clothing were everywhere.

The threesome spent several hours sifting through the wreckage, but found no CDs or anything that was even remotely related to the cyborg project. Essie and Botty had retrieved all of the items that were salvageable several days before and had them moved to the storage unit. There were some partially burned papers that were largely illegible, but most of the furniture from the first floor and almost everything that had been in the home had been reduced to ash. Rob was inconsolable.

"Boys, I am afraid of what Vladimir will do when I tell him that the cyborg plans have been destroyed in the fire," he said with an alarmed look on his face. "Vladimir's a nice guy as long as you don't get in his way," he added, frowning.

"What can he do to you, Rob? This isn't your fault. It was a horrible accident," Jeremy replied.

"I know Vladimir well enough to know that he'll do whatever it takes to get those plans. He may want to try reverse engineering..."

"Hey, wait a minute," Addison interjected with a look of concern. "The only way he could do that would be for him to take me to his lab and take me apart!"

"He wouldn't do that, would he Rob?" Jeremy asked incredulously.

"I can tell you he will try," Rob said, looking down at his shoes. "I think Bob and I signed something in that agreement . . . we never thought that *this* would ever happen . . . that Bob would die in a fire and the cyborg plans would be lost," Rob said sadly.

"We won't let anything happen to you, Addy!" Jeremy hurried to soothe Addison. "We won't, will we Rob?"

"Let's go home, boys," Rob said ruefully. "I can't think right now."

Addison was visibly shaken. He feared for his very life. Rob, Addison, and Jeremy returned home in silence. When they got there,

Essie and Botty were there to welcome them. "Any luck, boys?" Aunt Essie asked hopefully.

"No luck," Rob responded sadly, entering the house with the boys trailing behind him. They all fell into the living-room couch. Essie sat in a chair facing them, looking worried.

"Aunt Essie, Rob says Vladimir might try reverse-engineering Addison. They may take him . . ." Jeremy couldn't finish his sentence. He'd had so much loss in the last few years, and the thought of losing Addison too was just too much for him to bear. He got up and hugged his aunt tightly, burying his face in her neck.

Aunt Essie hugged Jeremy back. "We would never let them take Addy," Essie said softly. "Addy is an important part of our family now, not some robot they can just take apart like that."

"Thanks, Aunt Essie," Addison said, looking a little less scared. "This whole thing is like a nightmare," he added, looking concerned.

"We'll protect you, Addy," Rob said with authority. "We'll keep Vladimir away from you and keep you safe. Don't you worry."

"See?" Essie responded, smiling at Rob. "We're a family, Addy. All of us. Including you, Rob."

Rob smiled at Essie's comment. It made him feel very much a part of the Taylor clan.

"I promise, Addison. We won't let anything happen to you." Jeremy looked up, hopeful for the first time that he wouldn't lose his brother after all. "Bro, 'one for all and all for one,'" he said with a smile.

Essie and Rob nodded in the affirmative. They both seemed determined to do everything in their power to keep their newly formed family together and to save Addison Taylor from destruction.

CHAPTER 13

—————————— ■ ——————————

SPIRIT SPEAKS

L ater that evening, Jeremy and Addison went to Jeremy's bedroom to talk, brother to brother. "You know," Jeremy said, leaning back in his chair, "I didn't really feel like you were my brother until recently. But now I can't think of my life without you, bro."

"I know what you mean," Addison agreed, sitting on Jeremy's bed with his back to the wall. "Dad told me—you know, when I saw him at the funeral, and he said you were my brother, and to just be your friend—that things would work out between us. I wasn't so sure, to be honest. We're kinda different, you know? I mean, besides the obvious: you're human and I'm just a cyborg..."

"Addison, you are not '*just* a cyborg.' I think you are as human as human could be! But I know what you're saying. You're more of an intellectual, and I like cars and sports. Somehow, though, we connected, you know? Dad was right. It did kinda just work itself out."

After a while, Addison drifted off to sleep. Jeremy didn't want to wake Addy, so he covered him up and made up the fold-out couch on the opposite side of the room. He got some extra pillows from the closet, jumped onto the couch, reached for the light on the table beside the bed, and turned it out. He tried to sleep, but something was bothering him. He was tossing and turning. Jeremy was disturbed about losing his dad and by the thought of Vladimir coming over to get Addy to "reverse engineer" him.

Out of the blue, as Jeremy turned over to face Addy, his father suddenly appeared. He was iridescent, shining. He stood in between the boy's beds, and he was smiling. "Hi, son," he said. "Sorry if I scared you. I overheard your discussion with Addy, and I was so happy that you both feel as though you are brothers! It's exactly as I'd hoped." He sat down on the edge of Addison's bed. Addy sighed deeply and turned over, oblivious to what was occurring in the bedroom.

"Dad? Addison told me you came to him and told him you were okay, but I wasn't sure I believed him. I do now!" Jeremy sat up in bed, facing his father. "I'm glad you came, Dad. I wondered why you'd show yourself to Addy and not to me."

"Son, I had something I wanted to ask of him, that's all. I'm here now, though, as you can see."

"Yeah, Dad. I see you, all right. What's it like in heaven, and is Mom really all right?" Jeremy wanted some answers, and he hoped his dad would clue him in.

"Heaven's not what you think, son. But it is a fabulous place, filled with love—that's true. However, we don't sit around on clouds all day or anything. We do *work* there. I was working in a laboratory to help come up with a cure for cancer. Your mother is busy helping souls reintegrate to this higher level of existence after a stint on earth. You understand?"

"Sort of, but not really, Dad!" They both laughed. Understanding heaven would have to wait for Jeremy Taylor.

"Well, you'll understand when the time is right, Jeremy," his father concluded the subject. "I have some news for you, son."

"Yeah? What is it?" Jeremy was intrigued.

"I am coming back to earth—reincarnating—actually, right now," Bob responded in a serious tone. "I couldn't bear the idea of your being here without me, Jeremy. I know Essie, Rob, and Addy are your family now, but I want to be a part of it still, so I got permission to come back. I am reincarnating into Addison—I am giving him my soul. You know, a soul was the only thing I couldn't give him, and without that, well, he's really not human," Bob explained hesitantly. "The Powers That Be gave me the go-ahead to give him mine if I wanted to go back to earth. Your mother, by the way, completely understands and backs me up on this. She'll be there at home, waiting for us to return someday. I need to be with you, Jeremy. I want to make Addison completely human. I want us all to be a family again." Bob stopped talking, and looked into Jeremy's eyes. "Well, son, what do you think?"

"Dad, this is all very wild, you know? I don't really know what to think. Will Addison be you now? Will you be Addy?"

"As I understand it, Jeremy, we'll be one and the same. It's Addison's life, though. I'll be his light from heaven—his connection to the Source. I share my soul with Addison, and we learn together in this lifetime. When he dies, we both go to heaven as a combined soul."

"Dad, this is really, really freaky."

"Yes, I know, Jeremy. But I need to tell you, son, that when I enter Addison's body, I will no longer remember my last life, which means that I will not remember anymore that I am your father," Bob explained. "I'll simply be Addy. When we die, though, the memories do come back to our souls, so I'll remember our lifetime together then. Get it?"

"Dad, are you sure you want to do this?" Jeremy asked.

"Yes, Jeremy. I feel like my work is not done in this lifetime yet. I can't be happy in heaven with your mother knowing there's still more for me to do here," Bob said earnestly. "And I want to do this for Addy as well. I kind of feel I owe him this. I also want to be with you, Jeremy. I love you, son," Bob finished, giving him a kiss on the forehead as he always did.

"I love you too, Dad."

After father and son felt that they'd said everything they had to say, Bob's spirit rose up into the air. His body looked as if it were lying down, in the air. "Oh, and Jeremy." Bob had one more important issue he needed to share. "Please don't tell Addy that it's *my* soul he's getting.

I was told that he is not to know this at this time. The spirits made this very clear. Do you understand?"

"Yes, Dad. I won't let him know it's your soul he's got. But it *is* okay to let him know you were here and that he now has a soul, right?"

"That's exactly right. Thanks, Jeremy. I'll know you again as your dad when the time is right—on the Other Side. Until then, take care of yourself, Essie, and Addy, okay?"

"Absolutely. Bye, Dad."

"Bye, son." With that, Bob's spirit lowered itself into Addison's body. Addison shivered but kept on sleeping. Jeremy lay back down in his bed, thinking about what had just transpired. *Dad and Addy, joined together,* he thought. *Once Vladimir knows Addy has a soul, there's no way he will try to reverse-engineer him. He's human now.* Jeremy turned over, smiling. *I got my dad back,* his mind continued. *Well, sort of.*

CHAPTER 14

WHO'S WHO

The next morning was Sunday, and Jeremy had the day off work. It was late summer now, the sun a bit less intense, and Jeremy noticed this softening as the sun's rays streamed through his bedroom window. He hadn't slept a wink the night before, thinking about what had transpired with his dad. *Man, Dad's soul is in Addison . . . he is Addison . . . but not completely?* The thought ran through his mind over and over. *It's so hard to understand,* he surmised silently. *Souls reincarnating . . . life after death . . . wow!* Jeremy looked over at Addison, who was just beginning to stir.

"Hey, dude. How are you this morning?" Jeremy asked. Addison sat up in bed, rubbing his eyes.

"Well, to be honest, I feel kinda weird. Like something's . . . different. You know?" Addison shook his head.

"Addy, I have something to tell you," Jeremy began. "Dad was here last night."

"Really? What'd he say?" Addison came to full attention.

"He wanted me to tell you, well basically, that you now have a soul. He said he wanted to make you human—completely, you know? He knew if you could have a soul, you'd live forever, go to heaven and all, like us. That's why you feel different, Addy. You're one of us, now.

Completely and totally." Jeremy looked into his brother's eyes. "Kinda freaky, right?"

"Wow," Addison exclaimed, looking confused. "I never thought about life beyond this—what we have right now, you know? I am so happy you saw Dad last night and that he's happy. I guess I'll see him again now." Addy smiled. "This is a good thing, right?"

"Yeah, I think so," laughed Jeremy weakly. "We're brothers for life now—and beyond!"

"Whew, whew—scary, scary, bro! This is too much, even for me," Addy exclaimed, perplexed.

"For you? This is too much for *you*?" Jeremy retorted. "You should've seen me last night with Dad—I was completely blown away!"

"I bet you were!" Addison said and smiled. "This sort of thing doesn't happen every day!"

"Thank God it doesn't—I couldn't take it!" Jeremy exclaimed. "Well, do you want to tell Aunt Essie about this, or should I?" Jeremy wanted to know.

"Oh, I think it has to come from you," Addy said. "After all, you were the one who talked to Dad last night. I'm sure she'll want to know everything that happened. She'll be so happy to hear about this."

"Yeah, you're right," Jeremy said, throwing off the covers and standing up. "Let's go to the kitchen and see if she's up. Even if she isn't, I'm starved!"

"Right behind you, Jeremy," Addison said, getting out of bed and following Jeremy to the kitchen. "I'm kinda hungry myself!"

The kitchen was already lively. Rob was mixing some orange juice in a pitcher, while Aunt Essie was making breakfast on the stove. Sammy was lying on his bed by the stove.

"Morning, boys," Essie said in a singsong manner. "Would you two like some scrambled tofu?" she asked. "It's really good."

"Sure," Jeremy said, smiling. "That's one of my favorites."

"Me too," chimed in Addison. They sat down at the table, watching all the goings-on that went into breakfast at Rob's.

"Boys, coffee's made already. Help yourselves," Rob said. "Orange juice will be ready shortly."

Just then, Sammy got up off his bed and made his way to Addison's side. He wagged his tail and sat down, looking at the cyborg.

"He wants you to pet him, Addy," Rob said smiling. "Say, I think he finally likes you. I haven't seen him act friendly to you before."

"Me neither." Addison bent down to pet the animal, who was rubbing up against Addison's leg and enjoying the interaction.

"That's really weird, dude. He used to hate you, and now, for some reason, he likes you . . ." Jeremy's voice trailed off.

After breakfast was made and everyone had settled into the partaking part of the meal, Jeremy decided to broach the subject of the night before.

"Aunt Essie, Rob, I have something to tell you," Jeremy began, not really knowing how to say what he had to say without sounding incredibly weird. "Well, you know how Dad visited Addy at the funeral? I thought Addy was kinda crazy, you know? Well, he visited me last night."

"He did?" Aunt Essie asked, her eyes wide. "Really? What did he say?"

"He told me that he and Mom were okay, like he told Addy," Jeremy began. "Then he told me that he had gotten approval from heaven—from God, I guess, to get Addison a soul. He said that he'd always wanted to do that—to make Addy a real human—and that he was able to do it now. So Addy has a real soul now. He's as human as you or I."

"Wow," Rob said, furrowing his brow. "You know your dad and I did have conversations about just this very thing, Jeremy. Bob wanted to do everything in his power to make Addison a real human. He couldn't do that here, but I guess over *there*, you know, well, he has some sway in that arena." Rob laughed. "Your dad can be very persistent, if he wants to be!"

"So, you guys don't think I'm crazy?" Jeremy asked, looking back and forth at Essie and Rob.

"Of course not!" Aunt Essie exclaimed. "I know you, Jeremy. If your dad came and visited you and was able to give Addy a soul, that makes me very happy. Addy, you'll always be a part of this family now, even in the beyond. And even Sammy seems to know that Addison's changed." She leaned over her tofu and petted the dog who was still sitting next to the cyborg.

"I am glad we are a family—forever—too!" Addison replied, tears welling up.

"This is really amazing," Rob said. "I have to admit I was skeptical when Addy said he saw your dad at the funeral. But I truly believe you communicated with Bob last night. What he said to you, Jeremy—that's exactly what he'd say if he could, I know it!"

"Yeah," Jeremy replied. "He was like a dog with a bone if he needed something to happen." Everyone laughed. "Thanks, Dad!" Jeremy said, arms raised, looking up at the ceiling.

"Yeah, thanks, Dad!" Addy agreed. "I'm as human as I can be now, thanks to you!"

After breakfast, Addison headed back upstairs to change his clothes. Jeremy took that opportunity to sit down with Rob and Essie to explain more clearly what had occurred the night before. "Rob, Aunt Essie, there is a bit more to the story—but we can't tell Addy."

"Tell us," Aunt Essie asked, sitting back down at the kitchen table next to Rob.

"Dad gave Addy his own soul," Jeremy replied. "He said we couldn't tell Addy. He said it was part of the deal he made with the 'Powers That Be' where he was—in heaven."

"So your dad and Addison are—are the same being?" Rob was floored.

"Yeah, I guess. Isn't that wild?" Jeremy shook his head. "It's weird, Rob, really."

"This whole idea is going to take some getting used to, even for me," Aunt Essie responded, looking kind of dazed. "My brother and Addy are one and the same!"

"Don't forget—we can't tell Addy," Jeremy reiterated. "Promise me!"

Rob and Essie agreed that they wouldn't say anything about the situation to Addison. They all decided never to speak of the issue again.

CHAPTER 15

RUNNING SCARED

B right and early Monday morning, Rob entered Vladimir's office for their meeting as Vladimir had requested. Rob was nervous. Sitting in a chair opposite Vladimir's desk and waiting for the CEO to arrive was adding to his anxiety. *I don't know what I can offer him*, Rob thought, looking out the picture window at the city of San Jose and wishing he was anywhere but where he was. Just then Vladimir entered the room.

"Good morning, Rob," Vladimir said, closing the office door behind him. "I hope you have some good news for me." Vladimir sat down at his desk and looked Rob squarely in the eyes. "This cyborg endeavor has got to go forward. I already have a number of people and businesses interested in purchasing large quantities of them. This will be the biggest business opportunity for Human-istic, hands down!" he exclaimed.

"Yes, uh, about that," Rob began. "I can give you the specs for the cyborg brain creation, you know, with the computer chip and web download capability, but, um, I wasn't able to find the specs for the cloning effort."

"Rob," Vladimir stated, looking quite peeved, "this is not what I wanted to hear from you this morning. I have orders for this machine, and we need to get started manufacturing it as soon as possible. The

US Army is very interested in seeing our prototype, and the number of orders we could create for the company—with this client alone—is staggering. Have you looked everywhere possible for the plans, Rob? Because if we can't get the information from you very soon, I will be forced to take Addison and have him reverse-engineered. It could be, well, *not good* for him, and I would be saddened to have to take the machine from young Jeremy, considering the losses he's endured over these past several years. Do you understand?" Vladimir looked Rob squarely in the eyes. "You have twenty-four hours to produce the plans—*all* of the plans for this cyborg. Otherwise, I'll be forced to take Addison from you. By the way, this is in the contract that you and Bob signed. It's in the fine print.

"And Rob," Vladimir said, his voice softening, "you will be a very wealthy man once these cyborgs start rolling off the production line. You have a lot to gain here. You don't want to blow this, do you?" Vladimir stopped speaking, his eyes intent on Rob.

"Vladimir, I know I have a lot to gain. I *want* to give you all of the plans—I do. I will make every effort to get them to you by tomorrow morning. But taking Addison—that's crossing the line, sir. He's not a machine; he's actually human, Vladimir. I know you think I'm crazy for saying that, but take my word for it, because it *is* true."

"Well," Vladimir replied, sitting back in his black leather chair, "I can see you have bonded with Addison. To be frank, I think you've lost it here. You obviously aren't thinking very clearly. Where's your objectivity, Rob? Of course Addison isn't a human. Good God, you created him! You know better. Let's hope this little snag in our plans doesn't have a negative impact on young Jeremy, okay?"

"Yes, Vladimir. That young man is who I feel I have to protect. If he were to lose Addison now, I don't know what he'd do . . ." Rob's voice trailed off. "I'll just get going, then. I'll get back to you on this."

"You've got twenty-four hours," Vladimir stated again. "After that, I'll have to take things into my own hands."

With that, Rob got up from his chair and left Vladimir's office. He knew that even if he explained to him that Addison had a soul,

Vladimir would think that to be impossible and would consider him truly out of his mind. Rob wasn't even sure that Vladimir believed in souls in any case. *I've got to come up with something*, Rob thought. *I couldn't live with myself if Addison were . . . killed. It would be like losing Bob all over again.* He shook his head. Then he took the elevator down to the parking garage and drove home. *I have to find the schematics*, he thought, *or else, hide Addison . . .*

Rob walked into his house to find Addison and Essie working on some new yoga moves. "Hi, Rob," Essie greeted him, smiling. "You're home early."

"Yeah, I took the rest of the day off," Rob replied. He sat down and watched Essie and Addy work. "We have a problem," he added. "We have twenty-four hours to find the cyborg plans, or Vladimir will take Addison in to Human-istic and have him reverse-engineered. The money he stands to make on the cyborgs is too large; he won't let this go. He's already got orders for the cyborgs. He will do *anything* to get this cyborg project off the ground."

"Including taking our boy and doing anything they want to him? Well, they can't have him, Rob. That's it. We can't hurt Addison or Jeremy this way." Essie was visibly shaken.

"I think it would be prudent to find a hiding place for Addy," Rob continued. "Maybe someplace here in the house."

"How about down in the cellar somewhere?" Addison offered. "There are lots of little hiding places in the crawl space. I saw them when we were putting things in storage down there. I remember thinking it'd be a great place to play hide-and-go-seek with kids," he added.

"All right, let's take a look," Rob answered. The three of them walked in single file into the kitchen and down the stairs to the basement. It was cool and dark, partially submerged under the earth. The crawl space lay below half of the room and was only about four feet high. Rob went to his desk and took out some flashlights. "Here," he said, handing Essie and Addy each a light. "Let's get under there and see what's there." They crouched down, needing ultimately to get down on all fours and crawl around, with flashlights in hand, to light the way.

"Here," Addison said, pointing to an area near the corner of the house. "This place is great. I could hide behind all these Christmas decorations."

"This does look like a great hiding place. What do you think, Rob?" Essie asked.

"Well, we could put some sleeping bags down here, on an extra mattress I have, so he'd be comfortable . . . and maybe get some supplies—food and water—in case he needed to stay here for a while," Rob replied. Scanning the area, he added, "I think it's the best place down here to hide, Essie."

Essie looked pensive but at the same time a bit relieved to have found a suitable location in which to hide Addison. "Okay," she answered. "This'll be Addy's hideout."

They got out from the crawl space and trudged back upstairs. Essie made a list of supplies and other items Addison might need, should he have to stay downstairs for several weeks. When Jeremy came home from work, they let him in on the plan. Rob and Jeremy took Rob's car to the store and stocked up on the supplies necessary for Addy's indoor camping experience; then they went home to set up the hiding place for Addison. When everything had been put together, sleeping bags laid out, and food and water stored, Aunt Essie was finally at ease. "We'll keep Vladimir and his thugs out of here," she stated firmly. "We won't let them take you, Addison," she added, giving him a hug.

"Thanks, Aunt Essie," Addison replied, smiling at her. "This is great. I can stay down here in the cellar almost forever now."

"We'll say you went away," Rob added, "if they want to know where you are."

"We'll say you went to Mexico," Essie added. "And that you're not coming back."

"Sounds like a plan," Addison answered. "I think this'll work for a while."

"In the meantime, I'm gonna keep looking for those plans," Rob added. "Essie, I'm going back to work, to search Bob's office. I'll be back for dinner." With that, Rob headed up the stairs and out the door.

"Bye, honey," Essie said sweetly, waving good-bye.

That's interesting, Rob thought. *She called me* honey! He smiled to himself and then got in his car and drove off, feeling a bit happier than he had in a while.

CHAPTER 16

GET HIM!

B ack at Human-istic, Vladimir had gotten busy. He suspected that the plans for the cyborg were not forthcoming and that he would need to abduct Addison and reverse-engineer the young man. To that end, he had hired two "contractors," known only as Jeb and Wolf. Jeb was tall, well built, and had a buzz cut. He looked as if he'd been a marine at one time, although a Special Forces operator was not out of the question, Vladimir surmised as he welcomed Jeb and Wolf into his office. Wolf looked nothing like Jeb. Besides being in fantastic shape, Jeb was blond haired and blue eyed, while Wolf was of dark complexion, with black hair and eyes, and was pudgy around the middle. They took seats across from Vladimir. "You know why I asked you here, don't you?" Vladimir queried.

"Yeah, of course we do," replied Jeb. "Just give us the background info on the job," he added, looking intently at Vladimir.

"Here's some photos that I took recently of every one of the players in this scenario—actually, at a funeral," Vladimir replied, handing over the photos, "as well as the background story on each of them. Oh, and the addresses of everyone involved," Vladimir finished his thought. He handed the information to Jeb and sat down behind his desk.

"Now, I've given Rob—that's a picture of him there." Vladimir pointed him out. "I've given him until tomorrow morning to come up with the plans for the cyborg he created along with another scientist. This cyborg will be reproduced by my company. We stand to make a substantial amount of money on this venture." Vladimir grinned. "Anyway, the plans were burnt up in a fire—I lost an employee in that fire too—Bob. He actually was the brains behind the cyborg's creation. Bob was Jeremy Taylor's dad. There's a photo of Jeremy." Vladimir grabbed the photos from Jeb and sifted through them until he found a picture of Jeremy to show Jeb and Wolf. "And Jeremy, his aunt Essie, and the cyborg are living with Rob now. You guys should find Rob and tail him from now on—and then, if he doesn't come up with the plans by 9:00 a.m. tomorrow, I want you to go to his house and take the cyborg. I *know* he's there. His name is Addison, and this is what he looks like." Again, Vladimir grabbed the photos out of the hands of Jeb, found a photo of Addison this time, and pointed vigorously at him. "Bring the cyborg back here, and you get paid what we discussed over the phone. Remember—no cyborg, no payment. Got it?" Vladimir asked, pointedly. "Do whatever you have to do, but get that cyborg, alive, and bring him here. He's no good to me dead. And don't forget—he's a cyborg, so he's twice as strong and at least ten times as smart as you, for sure."

"Hey, that's not very nice to say about us, your new friends, Vladimir. I have a question. What about the others involved here?" Wolf asked, his eyes narrowing. "What if someone should, say, get in the way of us bringing that cyborg to you?"

"Well," Vladimir replied slowly, leaning forward on his desk, "if they get in the way, they may need to be taken out. Only in the most dire of situations, of course. I kinda like those guys."

"Extra to take them out. It'll cost another million to guarantee delivery." Jeb knew he had Vladimir over a barrel.

"Yes, fine; no problem," Vladimir replied quickly. "Just make it look like an accident, if something unforeseen should occur. Now, get out of here, and get to work."

"Yeah, we're outta here," replied Jeb. He and Wolf got up and left the office. At the same time, coincidentally, Rob had just gotten off the elevator. He was heading to Bob's old office to see if the cyborg plans might have been hidden in it somewhere.

"Hi," Rob said, acknowledging Jeb and Wolf.

"Hi," Jeb responded, smiling at Wolf. After Rob had passed them in the hallway, the two turned around and followed him to Bob's office. "I think this may be one of the easiest jobs we've had in a while," Jeb commented to Wolf as they walked down the hallway.

"Yeah," Wolf replied, rubbing his hands together. "We'll have to take a nice vacation to Cabo after this is over," he added, smiling wryly. "We'll be able to more than afford it."

CHAPTER 17

■

ADDY'S TRUTH

B ack at Rob's house, Addison had gone down into the crawl space to get himself acclimated. He figured he'd be spending a lot of time there, and he wanted to make himself comfortable. He had with him a blue cotton headrest, with pillows for support, and a small lamp that he had situated on a box with a table cover that he used for a night stand. Earlier, he had taken dozens of books from Rob's library and stacked them next to his makeshift bed. Addison loved to read, and Rob had a lot of technical books on a variety of topics, including cyborgs, that Addison was looking forward to consuming. As he sat on his mattress, looking at the book titles and thinking about where he'd like to start, his cell phone rang. It was Alex.

"Hi, sweetie," she said lightheartedly. "What are you up to?"

"Oh! Hi, Alex." Addison began to feel uncomfortable. Ever since his dad had died in the fire—and especially after that night when Jeremy had told him that he had received a soul—for some reason he couldn't explain, Addison no longer felt the same toward Alex. She felt more like someone he could care for as a friend. He had stopped thinking about her in a romantic way. He didn't know how he was going to explain it to her, but he knew that it had to be done.

"Alex?"

"Yes, Addy, what do you want to tell me?" Alex could feel that something important was on his mind. Addison had been acting more distant toward her, especially in the last several days.

"I need to explain something to you ... something weird," Addison began, with a pained expression on his face. The last thing he wanted to do was hurt her. "I've been going through some changes lately. I don't exactly know how to tell you this, but I feel differently toward you. I think it might have to do with that interaction Jeremy had with Dad since he died, but I'm not sure."

"What happened?" Alex was confused. "Jeremy saw his dad after he died? *Seriously?*" She hadn't heard about Addison getting a soul, because Addison hadn't thought she'd understand, and he hadn't known how to broach the subject with her. But he had to try.

"Well, Dad showed himself to Jeremy one night after the funeral. He told him that I had a human soul now, and that's what'll make me human, as opposed to being just a cyborg. When I woke up, I swear, I felt really different, but I couldn't put my finger on it. Anyway, after that happened, I didn't feel the same way that I used to about a lot of things, and my feelings changed toward you too. I kinda felt like I loved you like a girlfriend, Alex, I really did. But after that night, well, I still felt love for you, but more like love for a sister or a friend, you know? I don't want to hurt you, Alex, I really don't. I want us to be great friends. I still love everything about you, just in a different way—do you understand?" Addison was pensive. He hated having to tell Alex this, but it was time she knew how he felt, and it was the truth. He couldn't lead her on. It wasn't right.

Alex, sitting on her bed at home, was curled up close to her kitty cat. "Well," she started, "I have to say that I could feel things had changed between us on some level. Are you sure it isn't anything I said or did that made you change your mind about us as a couple?"

"Absolutely not," Addison answered. "You are and always will be someone very special to me. I'm the one who has changed. There are other things too ... that aren't the same with me."

"Like what?"

"Well, since Dad died . . . well, I like garlic now. Actually, I *love* it. Me! You know how I used to hate it? Now I can't get enough of the stuff!"

Alex laughed. "Well, that's a good thing, loving garlic. It's really not a great thing to live in the 'Garlic Capital of the World' and hate garlic!"

"I know, right? I also noticed that I don't seem to like sports anymore. Not at all. Me! I used to love playing basketball, and now, well, I'd rather read a book. And also, now I feel uncomfortable around people, whereas before I loved being with them all the time. What's up with that?"

"Do you believe in reincarnation, Addison? I do. Maybe you have a soul from a person who lived before who was more introverted. Bookish. That'd explain all the changes in you."

"I hadn't thought about that, but it would explain a lot. I'll have to ask Jeremy if he knows anything else about this soul of mine."

"Addy, do you want to know what the pastor at my church says about souls?"

"Sure. What?"

"He says that having a soul is a responsibility."

"Really? How?"

"He says they are a gift. From God. We're supposed to honor that gift by doing good works . . . and loving each other."

"Even the bad guys?"

"Well, maybe the bad guys should get some of that 'tough love' . . .

"I'd like to give Vladimir some tough love—right between the eyes!"

"Addison!"

"Sorry!"

"You really are human now, aren't you?"

"Yep. Alex, you need to know there are some creepy things going on with Vladimir. He knows that the cyborg plans went up in flames along with the house, so he's trying to get hold of me so he can do some reverse-engineering to find out how Dad made me. Essie and Rob have me in a secure location—I can't tell you where—until we can figure out what to do, so you won't be seeing me for a while."

"Addy, that's terrible! They could hurt you, or worse . . ." Alex trailed off.

"Don't worry, Alex. They won't find me."

"They better not."

"No, they won't. Please don't worry. I'll stay in touch when I can, okay?"

"Okay. And Addy?"

"Yes?"

"Be careful."

"I will. Bye, Alex."

"Bye, Addy."

Addison ended the call and put the phone down on the bed. He was relieved that Alex had taken it so well. He knew he'd always want her in his life but in a different way than before.

Turning to the situation at hand, Addison began looking through his pile of books and decided to read a book on ethics and cyborgs. *This one seems applicable to what's going on with me*, he thought. He smiled as he picked it up and started leafing through it.

On the other side of town, Al had just walked by his sister's room. He saw her there, cuddling her cat and looking thoughtful. Al backed up to stick his head into her room. "What's up, sis?"

"Addy just broke up with me," she stated. "Well, sort of. He still wants to be friends."

"You want me to beat him up or anything?" Al asked, looking upset. "I knew you were too good for him . . ."

Alex laughed. "Thanks, but no, bro. Please don't beat him up. I could tell things had changed between us, but I wasn't sure what it was. And now . . ."

"Okay, what is it? Inquiring minds want to know." Al sat down on the bed beside his sister.

"Jeremy had a discussion with his dad."

"His dad's dead, Alex."

"I know. He came to him—his spirit came, you know? Anyway, he told Jeremy that Addy had a soul now. That makes him human. We think Addy's soul has lived before, because he's not the same guy he used to be, get it?"

Al looked perplexed. "No, I have no idea what you just said! Sounds kinda creepy and weird to me. You sure you don't want me to beat him up?"

"Al! N-O! No beating anyone up. I think Addy's soul has been a live person before. You know, I think there might be something to us reincarnating after we die. It'd explain a lot . . ."

"Whatever you say, sis. Well, I think I'll just go to my room and play some video games. I understand video games!"

Al took off down the hall, shaking his head as he went, leaving Alex alone with her cat, Cuddles. "Well, Cuddles, it's just you and me again. We'll always love each other, the same today as tomorrow, won't we?" Cuddles purred, rubbing her body up against Alex's arm. Alex petted her, and Cuddles responded by arching her back. "*You* I get," Alex said, smiling.

Alex continued petting her cat, deep in thought. *I hope Addy will be okay . . . Vladimir better not hurt him . . . He better not touch a hair on his head, or so help me!* Her brow furrowed. *I hope that those terrible people at Human-istic never find him.*

CHAPTER 18

THEY'RE COMING FOR HIM

Jeremy and Casey had finished their workday at the auto-supply store and decided to get some pizza together. They headed for the nearest restaurant, a few blocks from the store, on foot. After they'd found a booth and ordered, Jeremy decided to let Casey in on the goings-on at home. "You know," Jeremy began, "Addison is not your average brother."

"I know," Casey replied offhandedly, taking a sip of her soda that had just arrived. "Addison is smart, funny, and an all-around great guy—of course, not as great as you." She gave Jeremy a huge grin, fingering the soda glass and rubbing off the condensation from the outside of the glass.

"Yeah," Jeremy began, "but he's more than that. Don't tell anyone, but my dad actually created him."

"Your dad created you too! What are you getting at?" Casey seemed confused.

"He's actually a cyborg," Jeremy said, gazing out the window. "At first he kinda pissed me off. He was just too perfect, you know?"

Casey nodded. "Yeah, my older sister Jenny is pretty perfect too, although she's no cyborg. But is it really true? Addy's really a cyborg?"

"That's just the tip of the iceberg," Jeremy said, turning and looking directly into Casey's eyes. "He's got an actual human soul.

My dad appeared to me several nights after he died, and he told me that Addison has a soul now and is as human as I am. And after that happened, Addy changed, and I think for the better. He's not Mr. Perfect anymore. He reminds me more of, well, my dad, now. But that's not even the most difficult part of the story. Vladimir, my dad's old boss, is trying to find Addy, so he can reverse-engineer him. My dad and Rob sold Vladimir the rights to the plans they created to make Addy, and they were burned up in the house fire. So Vladimir thinks it's okay to just kidnap Addy, because to him he's just a machine and not human. He wants to open him up and study him. There's no telling what Addy will look like or be like after that. So we're hiding him."

"You're kidding! No way! You're hiding him? Where?" asked Casey, understandably confused and alarmed.

"I'd rather not say. Rob thinks Vladimir will be sending people out to find him, no matter what the cost. Vladimir's company stands to make a fortune on these cyborgs. So if you knew where Addy was, you might be in danger." Just then their pizza arrived. Jeremy wasn't that hungry anymore, but he took a piece just the same. "I thought you should know what's going on," he continued.

"Jeremy, this is horrible! Is there anything I can do?"

"Not right now, but I'll let you know if anything comes up," Jeremy replied. "It's great just to be able to tell someone. Thanks for listening."

"Of course!" Casey moved closer to Jeremy on the semicircular cushion, leaned over, and kissed him lightly on the cheek. "I'm always here for you, Jeremy."

"Thanks, Casey," he replied, kissing her back. "That means a lot."

After they had finished their dinner, the two went their separate ways: Casey to the outlet stores and Jeremy back home to Rob's. As he was driving down the hill toward home, he noticed a black SUV parked in the circle above Rob's driveway. Two men wearing sunglasses were inside. The driver appeared to be reading a newspaper, and the passenger just stared out the window, watching Jeremy drive down the driveway. Jeremy parked his car and ran inside. "Aunt Essie? Aunt Essie!" he yelled. "Where are you?"

"I'm in the kitchen, Jeremy. What's up?" Aunt Essie was busy making a vegetable casserole. Jeremy ran into the kitchen.

"There are some weird-looking guys in a black SUV in the circle," he stated. "I wonder if they're looking for Addy?"

"Could be." Essie ran to the front living room window and peered out. "I haven't seen that car here before," she said hesitantly. "We'd better be careful. Be a dear and run down to the cellar and give Addy a heads-up." Essie ran to the phone and called Rob. "Honey, you'd better get back here now," she told him worriedly. "There are some guys in a black SUV watching the place."

Rob became concerned that his new family might be in danger. "I'm on my way, Essie. Don't go out. I'll be home shortly," he said, hanging up the phone.

When Rob arrived home, the SUV was still in the circle. The guy in the passenger's seat gave him a once-over, as he had Jeremy. Rob thought he looked familiar. As he got out of his car, he realized that he'd seen the guys earlier at Human-istic. As he entered his house, Jeremy and Essie ran up to him.

"What 'ya think?" Jeremy said.

"Have you seen them before? Do you know who they are?" Essie wanted to know.

"I did see the one in the passenger's seat before," he replied. "He was coming into Human-istic as I was leaving. I bet Vladimir hired them to watch the place and look for Addy. Does he know they're here?"

"Yeah, Rob, I told him," Jeremy replied. "He's on alert."

"Good." Rob gave a huge sigh of relief. "I didn't find anything else in Bob's office about the plans," he said, sitting down on the living room couch. "I gotta go in tomorrow and tell Vladimir that I've got nothing. Then, we all really have to be careful, because who knows what Vladimir is capable of? There's a huge amount of money at stake.

He's not going to just give that up. He's going to do whatever it takes to find Addy and open him up for inspection."

"Oh, Rob! This is horrible!" Essie replied. "Well, we'll all just stick to our story that Addy left town and we don't know where he went."

"Yeah," Jeremy agreed.

"I think that's best," Rob chimed in. "We must protect Addison at all costs."

CHAPTER 19

DANGER AROUND
THE CORNER

The next morning, Rob arrived at Human-istic a bit early. He got some coffee, sat back down at his desk, and tried to think about how Vladimir would take the news that there were no plans to be found. *Hope he won't kill me*, he thought worriedly . . . *I mean* really *kill me*! Just then Vladimir entered his office.

"Hi, Vladimir," Rob said nervously.

"Look, Rob, let's not screw around here. Do you have the plans today or not?" Vladimir sat down in the chair facing Rob and stared directly into his eyes. "Well?"

"Um, no, Vladimir, I don't have the plans. I can work up my part of the plans easily enough—"

"Well, sir, I think you'd better!"

"Okay, Vladimir. Done."

"I will need Addison to complete the plans. Don't worry, you'll get him back."

"Yes, but in what condition?"

"As good as possible."

"That's what I'm worried about." Rob sighed. "Vladimir, Addison is not just some machine. He's actually a human. He's part of Bob . . . and me. If you disfigure Addison, to me you are disfiguring Bob's memory. Don't you see that?"

"That's ridiculous! Addison is a *machine*! Yes, he has human DNA and skin, but other than that, he's a machine. He is 99.9 percent machine!"

"That's where you're wrong, Vladimir. So wrong. He couldn't be more human. In fact, well, he could be more human than you!"

"Rob," Vladimir said slowly and in low tones, "I don't know what you're trying to imply, but let's just leave that alone, for now. I think you're too emotionally tied to this project. You don't have the distance or rational judgment to be able to see the big picture. We create robots. We create cyborgs. We do not birth babies!"

"Okay, Vladimir, we're never going to agree on this."

"No, Rob. Sadly, we won't. You do understand, however, that you and Bob signed a contract with me. It says that I have the right to have Addison reverse-engineered in lieu of the plans being submitted to me. If you stand in my way, you are breaking the law."

"I never would've signed those papers if I'd known then what I know now!"

"Would've, could've—it makes no difference now." Vladimir leaned his elbows on Rob's desk and pointed his finger at him. "If you try to stop me from getting Addison, I can't be held liable for what might happen."

"Is that a threat, Vladimir?"

"Damn straight. I've got orders for this machine, and these orders come from the highest places in the US Government. We will get these plans, and we will make these machines. It's a matter of national security. You don't want to stand in the way of national security, do you, Rob?" Vladimir sat back in his chair, looking very satisfied. He'd made his point well. *How could Rob possibly stand in the way now?* he thought.

"You're going to hurt Addy," Rob replied. "We love him. He's part of our family. You'd be experimenting on a human being for profit."

"You'd better be careful and watch what you're saying, Rob, before you go too far!"

Rob seemed to see Vladimir for the first time. He suddenly realized that his boss would go to the ends of the earth to get these plans, no matter who he hurt.

"I think you better take the day off, before either of us says something we will regret," Vladimir continued. "Rob, go home. *Now!*"

Rob nodded his head, and Vladimir got up and stormed out of Rob's office. *This thing is getting very scary*, Rob thought as he put his work into his briefcase and left his office. *I've gotta get back to Essie, and Addy, and Jeremy. They're my family now, and they need me*, he surmised. *I love them all, and nothing will happen to any one of them if I have anything to say about it. But first I'd better stop off at the store and get some more supplies for Addison in his hideout. He may be stuck down there for a while.* Rob got in his car and sped over to the local food store, thinking about the new life he'd made and taking in the realization that they all meant much more to him than he'd previously known.

In the meantime, Jeremy and Al had decided to ditch class early and go to the hover-car racing rink. Jeremy needed to blow off some steam. "Thanks for coming with me, Al," he said, patting his friend on the back.

"Are you kidding? Like I need an excuse to race!" Al replied, hopping into the beloved yellow sports car that he enjoyed racing the most.

Jeremy hopped into his favorite red sports car, and the two made their way to the starting line. Al was to Jeremy's right as he revved the engine, and he glanced over to the other side of his car to see who else he'd be racing against. He began to tremble a little as he realized who was in the black roadster. The man looked like the driver of the SUV that had been in the circle at Rob's house.

"Hello, Jeremy," Jeb sneered, seeing the look of recognition on Jeremy's face. "I think we've seen each other before!" Jeb laughed out loud and revved his engine several times. "I'm looking for someone you know. Addison. Got any idea where he is?"

"No, I don't," Jeremy replied, glancing over at Al, who was fiddling with the instruments on his dashboard and not registering what was going on with his friend. "He left town a few weeks ago—"

"Don't you lie to me, kid!" Jeb was incensed. "We know he's around here somewhere!"

Just then, the starter began the countdown to begin the race. "On your mark ... Get set ... *Go!*" He dropped his black-and-white checkered flag. The race had begun. The dozen or so cars seemed to fly around the track at breakneck speed. Jeremy and Al dueled back and forth for first place. In the last lap, as Jeremy was coming into the final curve, he noticed the black roadster making an appearance to his right. Jeb's car moved up next to Jeremy's. He pulled his car up the side of the race course as far as he could and then slammed it with a massive force into Jeremy's car. The red sports car rolled over six or seven times, until it fell with a final thud into the middle of the course. The crowd was completely silent as they feared the worst.

"*Code Red!*" yelled the judge from the sidelines into the sound system. An ambulance raced to Jeremy's aid, just in time to pull him from the wreckage before the car burst into flames. Everyone at the track was in shock. Jeremy had been pulled out in the nick of time.

As the paramedics checked Jeremy's vitals, Jeb came walking up to the scene. "Jeremy, tell me where that cyborg is!" Jeb yelled in his face.

Just at that very tense moment, the judge made an angry announcement over the loudspeaker: "The maneuver by number thirteen has been deemed a one-eighty! The driver of the black roadster has committed this illegal act. Please evict the driver from this race course immediately," he commanded. Following the announcement, two security guards raced toward Jeb, each grabbing one of his arms. They began to escort him off the grounds. As Jeb was being led out, he turned and said in no uncertain terms to Jeremy that he wanted the cyborg and that he would get him "one way or another."

"Jeremy, are you okay?" Al ran up to his friend, who was sitting on a bed inside the ambulance.

"He's a bit banged up, but he's fine," one of the paramedics chimed in, jumping down from the back of the ambulance and patting Al on the back. "Don't worry. He's completely all right. He must have an angel watching over him," he added.

"I'll say," Al responded. Then, looking at Jeremy, he added, "Dude, you could've been killed! What happened?"

"That guy who hit me? He's looking for Addy. He was sent by Vladimir. He wants him bad," Jeremy said. He rubbed his knee. And I think this leg'll be sore for a while."

"So, did he try to—to kill you?" Al's eyes were widening.

"I don't think so. I think he was sending a message: 'Give me the cyborg, or someone will get hurt.'"

"Or killed! Oh, my gosh, Jeremy! What're you going to do?"

"Protect Addison," Jeremy replied firmly. "That creep isn't going to get him, and neither is Vladimir. Not if I can help it."

"Dude, you're brave . . ."

"Forget it," Jeremy said, hopping down out of the ambulance. "Let's go home. And Al? Don't tell Essie or Rob about this—they have enough to worry about right now."

The two walked slowly out to Jeremy's beloved Mustang. "This was a little more action than I bargained for," Jeremy said, smiling weakly. He had been banged up and shaken by the accident, and he was still somewhat in shock.

They both got in Jeremy's car, breathing sighs of relief. Each one knew that the events of the day could've turned much darker, and that luck—or something seemed to be on their side.

BRING HIM TO ME

B ack in his office after his argument with Rob and an in-depth discussion with his lawyer about the legality of the situation surrounding Addison, Vladimir decided to put in a call to Jeb. Jeb had gotten into his SUV where Wolf had been waiting at the race course and had just driven over to Rob's house to keep an eye out for the cyborg there.

"Jeb, you've got my go-ahead to do whatever you need to do to bring me Addison Taylor. Got it?"

"Got it, boss," Jeb replied. A look of evil satisfaction passed briefly over his face.

"So, have you seen Addison at Rob's yet?" Vladimir wanted to know.

"No, we haven't. But we let that kid Jeremy know that we want that cyborg. So far, he's not much help."

"Maybe you should pay Rob a visit. He should be on his way home now. I bet you could get some information about where Addison is from him. You know, you could lean on him a bit. I didn't get anything from him today. He thinks Addison is some Pinocchio, changed from a puppet to a real boy. What a sap."

"You've got that right, Vladimir. How could anyone believe a cyborg is human? Hey, Rob's just coming down the road. When he gets here, Wolf and I will go 'say hello,' if you know what I mean."

"Great, Jeb. Do what you have to. Get Addison and bring him to me."

"Don't worry, boss. We will."

As Jeb hung up the cell phone, Rob passed them and pulled into his driveway. He got out of his car and, leaving behind the supplies he'd just purchased for Addison, glanced at the two men and then walked hurriedly up the path to his home. He entered and shut the door quickly behind him.

"Let's go, Wolf. We have the boss's okay to have a 'little talk' with Rob about Addison's whereabouts."

"I love little talks," Wolf said, grinning. "Hey, can I have a little talk with these?" he asked, holding up his fists.

"Maybe so," Jeb agreed. "We'll see what we get from Rob the easy way first. But if he doesn't give us what we want, we may have to get the information the hard way."

Jeb and Wolf exited their car, walked down the driveway to Rob's house, and knocked on the door. When no one answered, they knocked harder. Botty answered the door. "May I help you?" the robot asked politely.

"Get outta the way, robot. Where's Rob?" Jeb pushed the robot out of his way and entered the home uninvited, with Wolf in tow.

"I was wondering when you guys were going to pay me a visit," Rob said, coming to Botty's aid. "Botty, you may go," he said.

"But sir, are you sure . . . ?" The robot looked over at the thugs and then back at Rob.

"Yes, Botty, I'm fine. You can go." With that, the robot turned and left the room.

"Vladimir wants us to ask you a few questions," Jeb said maliciously, looking around the living room. "Can we talk?"

"Guess I really don't have a choice in the matter," Rob answered, motioning for them to take a seat. Jeb and Wolf sat down on the couch, and Rob took a seat across from them.

"No one else is here, huh?" Wolf asked, looking around.

"You'd know better than me," Rob said uneasily. "You've been 'casing the joint,' as they say."

"Yeah, that's true." Wolf smiled. "Guess that Jeremy kid's not here—off workin' or learnin' stuff, I suppose," he added gleefully as Jeb nodded knowingly, "and the woman's off teaching her yoga, I bet."

"You guys got our lives down pat. So, what can I do for you?"

Down in the basement, Addison heard the muffled conversation going on upstairs and went to an air vent so he could hear what was being said.

"Well," Jeb replied, "we want to know where Addison is. We know you know, Rob. Don't give us any bull. Vladimir wants that cyborg. We were hired to deliver him. We will deliver him one way or another, if you get my drift."

"Addison left town without telling us where he was going," Rob replied. "He's not here. We haven't seen or heard from him in weeks."

"Oh no, Rob," Wolf said. He flexed his muscles, rubbed his hands together, and then made fists. "That just isn't true. We want the truth from you, Rob. Tell us where Addison is right now. You don't want me to become physical now, do you?"

"No, I don't."

"Too bad." Wolf reached over and grabbed Rob by the shirt. "Let's start this conversation again," he said. "Rob, where is Addison?"

Rob nervously glanced around, staring at the basement door. "Um, I don't know."

Jeb looked over at the basement door. "Hey, Wolf," he said, smiling. I think maybe he's down in the cellar."

"No, I told you—he's not here!" Rob said emphatically.

"Hmm . . ." Wolf looked at Rob's nervous-looking expression and then at the basement door.

"You know, Jeb," he replied, "I think maybe you're right. Rob, you stay here," Wolf commanded as he threw Rob back into his chair. "We'll be right back."

"I didn't say you could go down there!" Rob yelled as they opened the door and descended the stairs. Everything was quiet. Wolf and

Jeb methodically looked around, throwing boxes and other things around as they went. As they began looking under the crawl space, Rob appeared at the bottom of the stairs. "I want you both to leave my house now!" Rob was visibly upset, which let the thugs know they were onto something.

"I told you to stay upstairs!" Wolf was getting testy. "I think I'm gonna have to teach you a lesson." Wolf grabbed Rob by the neck, threw him down on the ground, sat on his chest, and began hitting him in the face. Blood began to stream from Rob's nose. He tried to scream, but the blood was also running down his throat, making that impossible.

Just then, Rob saw Addison coming out from the crawl space, looking angry. He grabbed Wolf's shoulders and threw him across the basement. Wolf hit the wall hard. The blow knocked him unconscious. "Get out of here!" Addison yelled, heading for Jeb.

"Hold on there, Addison," Jeb replied, smiling, knowing he had something that would have the cyborg over a barrel. "You don't want anything to happen to that kid, Jeremy, now do you?" Addison stopped in his tracks, staring at Jeb. Jeb had looked scared, but now he knew he had the cyborg. "Listen, kid. You want nothing bad to happen to Jeremy. *We* don't want anything bad to happen to Jeremy. And nothing will, as long as you come with Wolf and me to Human-istic." They just wanna run some tests on you—that's all. Then you can come back here and live happily ever after. No harm, no foul."

Addison knew the thugs had him. There wasn't anything he could do, without putting Jeremy in harm's way, and he wouldn't—*couldn't* let that happen. "Okay, I'll go with you, so long as you leave Jeremy, Rob, and Essie alone."

"Promise," Jeb replied. "We got no reason to. We were hired to bring you in for testing; that's it."

"No, Addy!" Rob had revived himself enough to stand. "Don't—"

"Rob, I have no choice!" Addison was firm. "I can't let anything happen to Jeremy. They'll never stop until they have me. I'm going with them. Besides, I'll be back after the tests." Addison looked upset and sad, as if he didn't know what else to do under the circumstances. Jeremy was his brother, and he had been put on earth to protect him. "Know I'll be okay, and I will be back," Addison said as Jeb, who'd revived Wolf, led him up the stairs.

Rob sat down at his desk, holding his bloody head in his hands. *Dear God, I wish I could do something,* he thought, sending out a prayer. *Please, God, be with Addison now. Keep him safe. He needs You now more than ever.*

CHAPTER 21

●

THE PLANS ARE...

Back at Human-istic, Vladimir was celebrating. Jeb had called him from the car, telling him that they'd found Addison and that he and Wolf were on their way to Human-istic with him. "I got some champagne for you guys," Vladimir exclaimed. He had a stash of top-notch California champagne chilling in a refrigerated case in his office for just such an occasion. He opened the case and took out a bottle of '65 Chandon, popped it open so that Jeb and Wolf could hear, poured himself a glass, and took a celebratory sip. "This is possibly the best champagne I've ever tasted," he said, inhaling the rich bouquet of the sparkling wine.

"Save some of that for us—and don't forget our checks," Jeb replied.

"Not a problem," Vladimir said, swirling his glass. "And I've got your checks right here. You've earned every penny. See you soon."

Vladimir hit the intercom button on his desk. "All engineers assigned to the Addison Project. Report to Laboratory number one in fifteen minutes. Specimen will be arriving shortly."

Vladimir put down his glass of champagne. He felt a sense of satisfaction and ease that he hadn't felt since his company's inception. His Botman 1000 had been an instant success, and the company had flourished. But then his competition had copied his success, and revenues weren't what they used to be. Now, with this cyborg, his fortunes were rising once again. He felt more in control of things. *I'll have what I need to proceed with the production of these cyborgs for our armed forces—and many others*, he thought. *The United States will never have to worry about having enough troops for war again. And Human-istic holds the patent. Billions of dollars doesn't even touch the amount of money we'll be making . . .* He had drifted off into a daydream about summer homes in France and Brazil when his intercom interrupted him.

"Vladimir, you have visitors here in the lobby. They are Jeb, Wolf, and Addison. Shall I send them up?" the receptionist asked.

"Escort them to Laboratory 1, and I'll meet them there," Vladimir responded. *Here we go*, he thought gleefully. Vladimir was waiting for them outside of the room as the receptionist and the threesome approached.

"You may go, Jasmine," Vladimir said, waving her away. She turned and walked back to her desk.

"Here he is, boss," Jeb said, smiling as he shoved Addison forward in front of him.

"Thanks for coming, Addison," Vladimir said. "We don't plan on hurting you, son. We will simply do some testing to find out what you're made of, so to speak." The other scientists were arriving at the lab, so Vladimir unlocked the door, and everyone entered. The scientists immediately went to work, readying the operating table, lighting, and instruments. Addison was alarmed. There were many implements that had blades and pointy metal objects on them. Vladimir saw Addison looking at them. "Son, we will be 'putting you under' during the operation. You won't feel a thing, I promise. It'll be over soon, and then you can go home to be with your family."

"I hope so, sir," Addison replied. "Jeremy, Aunt Essie, and Rob— they will be all right, no matter what, right? I mean, you wouldn't hurt them."

"Of course not. Your father's plans regarding your creation are all that I'm after," Vladimir responded. "Once I have them, we will begin production of the cyborgs, and Rob, Essie, and Jeremy—they'll all be rich. Believe me, this is win-win for everybody." Addison relaxed a bit at hearing that his family would be safe.

Meanwhile, Jeremy and Al had stopped at Gilroy High to collect Alex. "We gotta go over to Rob's and see how things are going," Al told her as she hopped into the backseat. "Some guys are looking for Addison, and they aren't fooling around."

"Oh my God! Let's go!" Alex replied as Jeremy sped off for home.

As he was driving up, he saw Rob run out of the house and jump into his car. "Hey, Jeremy!" Rob yelled. "Come quick. They have Addison!"

Jeremy slammed his car into park and ran over to Rob, with Al and Alex following behind. "Where? At Human-istic?" he asked.

"Are they going to hurt him, Rob?" Alex wanted to know. Her hands were beginning to shake.

"I'm not sure, Alex. I sure hope not," Rob replied; he was visibly upset as well. "I'm going over there to find out what's going on. Do you all want to come with me?"

"Yes! We have to save Addy," Alex said, looking at her brother, who nodded in agreement.

"You guys go with Rob—I'll take Botty. He's faster!" Jeremy ran into the house and brought Botty out. The robot changed into his motorcycle self, and Jeremy grabbed his helmet from the backseat of his car, swung onto the robot, and the two sped off in the direction of Human-istic.

Shortly thereafter, Rob took off with Alex and Al in the backseat, speeding around the country roads toward his office. When they arrived, they saw Botty standing outside waiting for them.

"Jeremy's inside already," he stated, pointing to the front of the building.

"Thanks, Botty," Rob replied, running past the robot with the twins in tow. The three entered the building and ran to the receptionist's desk. "Where's Addison?" Rob asked the receptionist, somewhat out of breath.

"In Lab 1," Jasmine said, nodding toward the entryway to the labs. "Shall I announce you?"

"It's not necessary, Jasmine," Rob responded hurriedly. "They're with me."

"Rob, you need your guests to have badges! They can't just enter—come back here!" When they didn't stop, Jasmine called security. Two men with guns ran down the hallway after them.

Rob, Al, and Alex sprinted down the hall, with Rob in the lead. He slowly opened the door to the lab, and there he saw Addison on the operating table in the middle of the room, out cold, his newly shaven head wired with electrodes. A scientist was probing different areas of his brain. There was an anesthesiologist monitoring his breathing. Vladimir and a group of scientists were sitting in the front row of seats surrounding the table in the small, intimate theatre that was Lab 1.

Jeremy—who had snuck into Human-istic when the receptionist wasn't looking, had found Addison in the lab and had been quietly making his way toward his brother with the idea of grabbing the probe from the scientist's hand—was very relieved to see his friends. "Rob! They're operating on Addy—we have to stop them! <u>Now</u>!" Jeremy angrily grabbed the electrodes off Addison's head. "Leave my brother alone!" he screamed. Just at that moment, Addison began to speak.

"Hey, Rob, son . . . Hi, Al and Alex . . . Jeremy, my boy, how are you doing?" The voice was familiar, but it wasn't Addy's. Everyone looked perplexed, except for Jeremy.

"Dad! Dad! It's you!"

"Yes it's me, son!" Then, turning toward the surgeon, eyes closed, Bob-as-Addison commented, "John, with that probe of yours you just found the part of the brain that houses the soul—congratulations!" He smiled. "You didn't believe in a soul, did you, John?" Bob queried the lead scientist on the project, whose name *was* John.

"How—how do you know my name?" John asked, somewhat disbelievingly.

Just then, four security guards dashed into the lab and grabbed Rob, Al, Jeremy, and Alex. "What would you like us to do with them?" queried the lead security guard.

"It's okay, Frank. You can let them go. I don't think they'll be a problem," Vladimir answered, surveying the scene. The group was looking somewhat dazed. "But stay close by. Just in case."

"Call me if you need me," Frank responded, reluctantly letting go of Rob's arm. "Come on, boys." The other security guards followed suit, and they all left the room. Rob, Jeremy, Al, and Alex surrounded Addison quietly, watching the scene intently.

"To answer your question, before we were so rudely interrupted, we've worked together for years, John," Bob-as-Addison continued, still under anesthesia. "Remember the Johnston Project last year? I thought you were going to lose it then for sure; you got so mad when we were having such a hard time making that robot—"

"Bob? Is that really you?" John asked, dumbfounded.

"It's me, believe it or not!" Bob replied. "Hey, Rob," he said, motioning toward his old friend. "Thanks for taking care of things for me. I really appreciate it," Bob said through Addison.

"Um, Bob, buddy, I miss you," Rob replied, tears welling up. "I really wish it could be . . . the way it was . . . before the fire," he said.

"Well, buddy, I miss you too. You're one heck of a guy. By the way, I want you know if you and Essie were to get married—just sayin'— that'd be okay with me." Addison smiled slightly, and Rob thought he looked just like Bob used to when he was giving his old friend a hard time.

"We'll see about that!" Rob responded, smiling back.

"Vladimir?" Bob said, looking more serious through Addison's facial expression. "You don't need to do any more work on Addy. There is a copy of the plans in a manila envelope that wasn't destroyed in the fire. Everything you'll need is in that packet; with that information, you'll be able to make as many cyborgs like Addison as you want."

"Bob? This isn't happening—this can't be! It's gotta be some kind of trick!" Vladimir was dumbfounded.

"Vladimir," Bob said slowly, "remember when we went camping back in '82 in Yosemite, and we discovered that pristine lake that no one had ever seen before? You said it was the most amazing thing you've ever experienced. It was just you and me there, pal."

"Oh my God—Bob?" Vladimir was flabbergasted.

"Yes, Vladimir, it's really me. I want you to understand that I gave my heart and soul to the creation of Addison—so much so that God permitted me to give my actual soul to him. I couldn't leave Jeremy without a parent, and I didn't want Addy to be a soulless cyborg—so here I am!" Bob exclaimed.

"Also, Addy doesn't know I gave my own soul to him, and when this experiment is over, I won't remember being Bob anymore. I am now very much living the experience of Addison Taylor. We are one."

"Okay, okay," Vladimir replied, collecting himself. "I don't know what's going on here, but let's just say that you *are* Bob. Bob, where are the plans for the cyborg?"

"In the sock drawer in my dresser," Bob replied offhandedly. "Jeremy, you know I always put my most important things there, right?"

"Dad, I completely forgot. I guess I just didn't think . . ." Jeremy replied, sheepishly.

"Son, there's been a lot going on in your life. I think you can be forgiven! This is what I want you to do—go to the storage room where the furniture is being kept and look in my dresser drawer. You'll find the plans there."

"Thanks, Dad; I will."

"And Jeremy, give those plans to Vladimir. He has a right to them," he went on. "This is the way things are supposed to be. It's part of the universal plan. You'll find out what I mean soon enough."

"Yes, Dad," Jeremy replied. "I promise to give Vladimir the plans."

"And Dad?"

"Yes, son?"

"I love you, Dad," Jeremy said, tears streaming down his face now as he looked at Addison on the table.

"I love you too, son," Bob replied. "And Jeremy, you can tell Addy about his soul now. Understand?"

"Understood, Dad."

"Okay, everyone. Let's stop for the day." John had had enough of what was happening in that room. Vladimir agreed. It was time to stop the work on Addy.

The scientists began putting things away, except for John, who stitched up Addison's head. They took him off the anesthesia and left him on the gurney until he awoke from the drug-induced stupor.

"Jeremy?" Vladimir said, turning toward him. He looked pale. "I don't know what's going on here, but something is telling me that those plans exist. Will you go and look to see if they are in that sock drawer, and bring them to me if you find them?"

"Yes, Vladimir. I promised Dad that I would. I'll go right now."

"Great. We'll just hold onto Addison here until you get back. Um, just to make sure—"

"I *will* be back," Jeremy replied, feeling some anger welling up.

Rob, Al, Alex, and Jeremy headed for the car. The robot was standing by the car, waiting for them. "Get in the car, Botty," Jeremy commanded. "We have some work to do."

"Is Addison all right?" the robot wanted to know.

"Yes, he'll be fine. We have to go to the storage room where our old furniture is. Apparently there is a copy of the cyborg plans in Dad's old sock drawer," Jeremy replied.

"How do you know that?" Botty asked, getting into the backseat of Rob's car.

"It's a long story, Botty," Jeremy sighed. "When we come back here with the plans, Vladimir will give us Addison." He then got into the passenger's seat.

After everyone had put on their seat belts, Rob started the car and slowly headed out of the parking lot. "Boy, that experience was one for the books," he said. "I really don't know what to make of it."

"Hey, I just realized something—I was dating your father, Jeremy!" Alex said from the backseat, looking perplexed. "Boy, this is some wild world!"

"Too much for me," Al said shaking his head. "You guys are all crazy, you know that?"

Everyone laughed as they sped off toward the storage garage. "I really hope those cyborg plans are in that sock drawer," Rob said.

"They are," Jeremy said, smiling. "Dad *said* they were!"

CHAPTER 22

·

LOST AND FOUND

I t took just a few minutes for Rob to get to the storage garage. There was only a paltry amount of furniture and other goods the Taylors treasured that had been undamaged by the fire. Rob had the keys to the unit, as he'd gone there several days ago to look for the cyborg plans. Jeremy told Rob he wanted to go in alone first. Rob was fine with that, and the twins understood. Jeremy needed some alone time with the stuff of his past.

As Jeremy entered the garage storage space, he felt a sense of nostalgia wash over him. There, before him, were so many of the things that he'd grown up with: old toys, furniture items from when he was a child, and pictures that had been in the living room in his younger years, including old wedding pictures of his mom and dad. He sighed. *I so miss Mom,* he thought as he rummaged through all her old belongings that his dad hadn't been able to part with. Clothes and shoes that she had worn still smelled a bit like lilac, her signature scent. Jeremy inhaled the flowery smell deeply, trying to memorize it and take it into the core of his being.

Then he saw what he and his friends were looking for—his dad's old dresser. It was a large antique oak dresser that was tall and had a unique presence to it, as if it had seen so much in its day.

Jeremy pulled open the dresser drawer that was the second from the top—the sock drawer—and was surprised by what he saw. Besides many pairs of socks that had been folded neatly, there were a lot of old pictures—mainly of *him*. There were pictures of when he was born and when he'd learned to ride a bike for the first time.

Additionally, there were pictures of when Jeremy's mother had taken him to school on his first day of kindergarten. He smiled, remembering how scared he had been. But his Mom had made it all okay. She had always made things okay. Jeremy sighed. The many memories of his childhood were rushing back.

Also, buried deep in the drawer, was a little baggy with an old tooth of his. *I had no idea Dad had all of this,* he thought to himself. *Why Dad would keep this, I have no clue!*

Then, all the way at the back of the dresser drawer, he saw the manila envelope. He took it out and opened it. Inside, there was a disc and what looked to be a hard copy of the plans to make the cyborgs. He grinned. *I knew Dad was telling us the truth!* he thought triumphantly.

Just then, Rob peeked into the garage. "Everything okay, Jeremy?" he asked with concern.

"Rob, I found the plans!"

"Oh my God, Jeremy! That's great!"

Al and Alex heard the exchange and came running. "Jeremy, you found them?" Al asked, running inside the garage and grabbing Jeremy's arms.

"I did. They're right here, in this envelope. Everything's here, Rob. The plans are on this disc, I think, and there's a hard copy here too."

"Let's get back to Human-istic," Alex said excitedly. "We have to rescue Addison." Everyone agreed.

Rob drove back to the office, with the teens talking back and forth excitedly about the find. Botty looked at each one in turn as they animatedly discussed what had just transpired. "Stay here, guys," Rob said, when he'd parked the car in front of the building. "I'll be right out with Addy."

Inside Human-istic, Vladimir was waiting in his office. Rob walked inside and sat down in the chair across from Vladimir. "They were there, Vladimir. All this time. Anyway, here are the plans. There's a disc inside and a hard copy as well."

Vladimir opened the envelope and smiled. "All right, Rob, it looks like everything's here. Addison's in your office waiting for you. I knew you'd be back for him. Of course, if there are any hiccups here, I'll have to take him back, but things look fine at this point. You should be happy, Rob. We have the plans now, you have Addy, and we're all going to become very, very rich!"

"I'm just happy to be getting Addy back right now," Rob replied.

"Yes, I guess you would be," Vladimir said. "But the money won't hurt, you know." They shook hands. "I'll see you Monday morning, and we can talk more," Vladimir said as he walked Rob to the door. "Take the rest of the week off."

"See you then, Vladimir," Rob replied.

After leaving Vladimir's office, Rob ran down the hall to his own office. He opened the door, and he saw Addison reading one of his books on software design. "Doing some light reading, son?" he asked.

Addison turned around, dropped the book, and ran into Rob's arms. "Can we go home now?" he asked.

"Yes, Addy, we're going home. Jeremy found the plans that Vladimir needed, and I just gave them to him. He says we can go home now. Jeremy, Botty, Alex, and Al are in the car waiting for us." They walked together down the hall and outside to the car, where the teens were waiting. Upon seeing Rob and Addison, the teens got out of the car and ran to Addison, tears streaming down their faces.

"I'm so happy you're okay, dude!" Jeremy said, hugging his brother as hard as he could.

"Me too!" Addison agreed, hugging him back. The twins threw their arms around both of the boys, adding to the jubilation.

After they'd calmed down, everyone piled into Rob's car for the ride home. Jeremy and Botty rode in the front seat with Rob, while Alex sat on one side of Addison and Al on the other in the backseat.

The car was quiet as they drove home, each person processing what had just transpired. After a while, Jeremy spoke. "Addy, I have something to tell you," he began, somewhat haltingly. "The soul you got is Dad's. He didn't want to leave me here without a parent, and he didn't want you to be soulless. The Powers That Be allowed him to give his soul to you. I wasn't supposed to tell you about that, until now."

Addison thought for a moment. "That explains a lot, Jeremy. My personality changed, and I wasn't sure why. I'm more introverted than I used to be—and I like garlic now!"

The car filled with laughter as the teens recalled the first time Addison had taken a mouthful of the garlic ice cream at the Gilroy Garlic Festival.

"That also explains why you broke up with me," Alex added, giving Addison a hug. "We just weren't meant to be together. Given you have Mr. Taylor's soul, us being a couple would be just—just *creepy*!"

After Rob, Botty, Alex, and the boys had arrived back at Rob's home, Essie insisted that they go out to Mario's for a nice Italian dinner to celebrate Addison's coming home and the finding of the cyborg plans. The restaurant was homey and welcoming.

"This was a great idea, Aunt Essie," Addison exclaimed as he took a large forkful of pasta into his mouth. "The food's awesome, and I love this place."

"This *was* a great idea, honey," Rob added.

"*Honey?*" Alex asked, looking up from her plate of lasagna. "Is there something going on here we should be aware of?" she asked, smiling.

Rob blushed, sipping his glass of Chianti. "Well, maybe so," he said shyly.

"Maybe? Are you kidding?" Jeremy chimed in. "You two have been lovey-dovey for months!"

"We kinda fell in love," Aunt Essie said, putting down her fork. "It wasn't planned; it just happened."

"Yes, we did," Rob agreed happily. "Except I've been in love with you forever."

"You have?" Essie asked, surprised. "I didn't know that."

"Since the first time I met you, dear," he replied, putting his arm around her.

"Well, I don't know about that, but I do know that I love you right here, right now!" Essie replied, giving him a big kiss on the lips.

"Whoo, whoo!" the kids said, whistling at them and grinning ear to ear.

"Okay, that's enough of this," Rob said, smiling. "Let's have a toast. To love."

"I like that!" Essie said, raising her glass. "To love!"

Everyone clinked their glasses together. "I feel like things are going to be okay now," Jeremy said, smiling.

"Me too," Addison agreed. "As long as we're all together, things will be awesome."

CHAPTER 23

•

TYING THE KNOT

A few months later, just as the winter holiday season was getting underway, Jeremy and Addison were helping Rob put up the Christmas lights on the outside of the house. "This is such a festive time of year," Rob said, hammering some of the lights up along the eve of the garage. "I love celebrations," he added, looking at the boys. "Don't you?" Both Jeremy and Addison nodded affirmatively. "You know what?" Rob continued. "I think we need more celebrations! Tell you what, let's leave this for a while and go inside for a moment." The boys followed Rob inside. Essie was busy putting up the Christmas decorations in the living room.

"Essie?" Rob said, taking a seat by the Christmas tree.

"Yes?"

"Come here for a moment." Rob smiled as he picked up a small wrapped package from under the tree. Jeremy and Addison sat down on the couch nearby. "Jeremy, Addy, and I were just thinking that we need more celebrations. I thought we could start right now," Rob said. Essie looked into his eyes, not knowing what was up.

"Okay . . . what kind of celebration do you have in mind?" Essie asked as she came to join Rob by the tree.

"You'll see," Rob responded, handing Essie the package. "Consider this an early Christmas present," he continued. Essie sat down on the ledge by the fireplace.

"Go ahead, open it!" Jeremy exclaimed; he was getting increasingly excited for his aunt.

As Essie opened the package, a look of uninhibited happiness crossed her face. Inside sat a beautiful ring, with a five-carat round blue diamond, in a simple gold setting. "Is it—?"

Rob got up from his seat, and knelt down in front of Essie, who was beginning to tear up. "Essie Taylor, will you do me the honor of becoming my wife?" he asked, taking her hand.

"Yes, of course I will!" Essie replied, throwing her arms around Rob's neck and kissing him passionately. Addison and Jeremy howled and clapped.

"Welcome to the family," Jeremy said. "I mean *formally*, of course, Rob."

"Yes," Addison added. "Looks like you will be the newbie of the family now," he went on. "I'm just old news!"

"When are you going to tie the knot?" Jeremy asked.

"Well," Rob answered, "Essie, I was thinking we could get married in between Christmas and New Year's. I already checked with the church, and they can do the ceremony. Can we do it in a couple of weeks?"

"Sure we can!" Aunt Essie exclaimed, grinning from ear to ear. "I already had my eye on a wedding dress I saw in this small shop in Santa Cruz. One hundred percent organic cotton dress, and white slippers that match perfectly—you know, just in case!"

Rob had more to say. "And Essie, I spoke with Vladimir about our possible upcoming nuptials, and he wants to throw us a reception at his mansion in San Martin. He has a great room that would be perfect for a party. He wants to make amends for the trouble he's caused us."

"Rob, I don't know. I don't trust that man." Essie looked troubled.

"But, dear," Rob countered, "don't we have to give him the benefit of the doubt? We got Addison back in one piece, he's got the cyborg plans, and we're all going to be rich. Your brother told us to give him the plans, Essie."

"Well, that's true. I guess I should let bygones be bygones. No harm was actually done. Okay, let's do it!"

Essie looked happier than Jeremy had ever seen her. In fact, she was glowing. He was truly happy for his aunt and Rob. If he had to have a new uncle, he was glad that it was Rob.

Several weeks later—after a Christmas that was full of great cheer and more than a few presents—the wedding between Aunt Essie and Rob took place at the local Presbyterian Church. Essie looked beautiful in her long white cotton gown, and Rob looked dapper in a black-and-white tux. Jeremy was the best man, and Addison gave the bride away. The ceremony went off without a hitch, so to speak, and afterward, the happy couple and guests all drove to Vladimir's expansive home at the top of a hill overlooking the valley.

Vladimir's home was huge and palatial, as advertised. The "great room" really was great, as it had high ceilings, with gold floor-length curtains that covered ten-foot-high glass doors running the length of the ballroom. The curtains were pulled back, exposing a beautiful vineyard that cascaded down the long slope from the house. At the end of the vineyard, there was a two-story circular stone building, where the grapes were pressed and the wine aged in oak barrels before it was bottled. Vladimir made wine as a hobby, and he specialized in Cabernets and Merlots. He had his own label too, with his picture on the front and his last name, Petrov, emblazoned across the top. He had bottles of his wine on all of the tables for the guests.

Additionally, Vladimir had hired a popular local band for the occasion, who played "soft rock" love songs for the couple. He had also arranged a catered dinner that included some of the best roast beef regionally, vegetarian lasagna (for Essie, mostly), a variety of salads, caviar, and shrimp.

The dance floor was packed with the couple's friends, family members, and work acquaintances, who were taking pleasure in the festive occasion. Jeremy had invited Casey to be his date, and they thoroughly enjoyed the time they had together that evening: Jeremy even danced with her, to her delight, though he obviously seemed ill at ease. She appreciated the effort.

Of course the twins were there, and they had a great time as well. "Wow, Vladimir really knows how to throw a party!" Al crowed; he was filling up on the caviar. "This is awesome!"

In the meantime, Jeremy was dancing with Casey to the beat of some old '40s tunes the band was serving up. "I don't know what I'm gonna say—I mean, when I give the toast," Jeremy said nervously. "Should I tell everyone about how Rob has been friends of the family forever?"

"I wouldn't," Casey replied, dipping and dancing closely with Jeremy. "They don't want to hear a whole story. Just say what you feel—from the heart, you know?"

"Yeah, I guess so," Jeremy replied. "Thanks, Casey. That helps."

"Jeremy?" Casey twirled around and then grabbed her partner, pulling him close. "I have a question."

"Shoot, girl."

"Well, I've always wondered . . . what does the *Q* in your name stand for?"

"You mean, what's my middle name?

"Yes. Can you tell me?"

"Well, I usually don't tell. I kind of keep it to myself, mostly. It's kind of a secret."

"But you'll tell me, right?"

Jeremy sighed. "Well, I guess so. Since we're dating and all. The *Q* stands for 'Quirk.'"

"*Quirk*? Really? Why?"

"Well, it was my mother's maiden name. It's Irish. It means 'peculiar' or 'a sudden twist or turn.'"

Casey giggled. "That's so funny. I mean, not that the name is funny, exactly. *Peculiar*? Yes, you're a little weird. But that second meaning? It so-o-o fits you!"

Jeremy smiled. "Yeah, I guess it kind of does, doesn't it? I'm full of sudden twists and turns!" And with that, he twirled Casey around and around. Then he turned himself around and grabbed her from behind, swaying them both back and forth.

"That was bad, dude!" Casey smiled. "You know, Jeremy, you're a lot of fun. I kind of like you!" Casey turned toward him and kissed him on the cheek.

"The feeling's mutual, girl!"

Back on the sidelines, watching his brother and Casey dancing, Addison was also surveying the goings-on in the ballroom and happened to look over at one of the tables near the dance floor. He noticed that Amanda was sitting there alone. She was looking longingly at the dancers. Addison strode over to her table. "Hi, Amanda," he said. "Nice to see you." He offhandedly glanced down at her hands. She was nervously twirling a gold ring on her finger.

"Hi, Addy."

"I didn't know you were married," Addison said, looking perplexed. Amanda had always seemed to be coming on to him in yoga class.

"Oh, you mean the ring. I *was* married. My husband, Marty, passed away several years ago."

"I'm so sorry, Amanda. I didn't know." Addison was genuinely moved.

"It's okay. It was a while ago now. Marty would've loved this reception. He loved to dance . . ." Her voice trailed off.

"Amanda, may I have this dance? I enjoy dancing as well." Addison held out his hand.

"Addy, you don't have to—"

"No, Amanda, I *want* to," Addison stated, and to his surprise, he meant it. Amanda took his hand, and they headed for the dance floor. The band was playing something slow. Addison put his arms around Amanda and they began to dance. Addison smelled her golden hair, and he thought it had a scent of honeysuckle. He liked it. The band played another slow tune, and the two continued dancing, in a state of suspended animation, it seemed. They were in their own little world—at least for a while.

CHAPTER 24

───────────── ■ ─────────────

ENDING OR BEGINNING?

The wedding reception was ramping up, with everyone having a good time. Then the happy newlyweds entered the ballroom, to a barrage of applause from the many happy, smiling well-wishers. Rob and Essie took their places at the head table, followed by their tablemates. The head table was situated right in front of the dance floor, and it included Jeremy and Casey, the twins, Botty and Addison, and the newlyweds themselves.

When everyone was seated at their tables, Jeremy stood up and raised his glass. The guests began clinking theirs with their knives, until the crowd became quiet. "I'd like to make a toast," he began, nervously. "To my aunt, Essie, and my new uncle, Rob. After my parents died, they didn't hesitate. They took care of me. They made me feel loved. I am so grateful and so very happy that they fell in love and are now married. They are the most wonderful people . . . and they found each other. I know they will be the couple that will live happily ever after, as they say in the fairy tales. To Aunt Essie and Uncle Rob!" Everyone clinked glasses and drank to the happy couple.

"That was great, Jeremy," Casey said, giving him a kiss.

"Thanks, son, that means a lot," Rob chimed in.

"Jeremy, that was beautiful," Aunt Essie added, tearing up.

"Okay, let's eat!" Jeremy said, changing the subject.

"I agree—I'm starved!" Addison added.

Jeremy filled his dinner plate with lots of roast beef, as did Addison. Jeremy leaned over his aunt and Rob to talk to his brother. "Don't you just love roast beef? It is so-o-o good!" he exclaimed, taking another bite.

"You ain't kiddin', bro," Addison whispered back, while smiling at Essie.

"Well, you boys better enjoy that roast beef, because there won't be any of that when I get back from the honeymoon!" Essie said passionately.

Just then Vladimir came up to the table. "Is everything to your liking, Rob?" he asked.

"Everything's great, Vladimir," Rob replied, smiling. "I can't thank you enough for this."

"No problem," Vladimir answered. "I'm just glad we can put all that unpleasant stuff behind us and concentrate on a bright future for everyone," he finished. At that moment, Vladimir's butler, Jonathan, entered the ballroom. Upon spying his employer, he made his way to the head table.

"Excuse me, sir, but you have some guests waiting for you in the study."

"Thank you, Jonathan; I'll be right there." Vladimir surveyed the head table and the reception, taking pleasure in the fact that the party was being so well received. "Well, duty calls. No rest for the weary and all that . . ."

"Yes, please don't let us keep you from your business," Essie said. "Vladimir, I want to thank you, from all of us," she continued while looking at the boys, "for your hospitality."

"It's the least I could do, Essie," Vladimir replied. "Party on!" Vladimir then waved good-bye and headed for the door.

"It really was nice of him to do this for us," Essie continued. "He didn't have to do it."

"That's right, dear," Rob said, taking her hand and giving it a gallant kiss.

"Well, I still don't trust him," Jeremy said.

"I have to say that the jury is out on Vladimir Petrov," Addison chimed in.

Vladimir entered his study to find Wolf and Jeb sitting by the fireplace. A huge fire was roaring, and they were warming their hands. "This is nice," Jeb said as Vladimir entered.

"It's real cold outside," Wolf added. "We prefer the warm weather."

"Glad to hear that," Vladimir said, taking a seat nearby. "You two did such a great job on the Addison thing that I was thinking I might be able to use you on another project I'm working on."

"Yeah?" Jeb asked, his interest piqued. "What kind of project?"

"Well, if I gave you the specifics right now—well—I'd have to kill you," Vladimir replied, an evil grin beginning to show on his face. "Cigar?" Vladimir opened a cedarwood box on his desk that held Cuban cigars. "They may not be legal, but they are superb." Jeb and Wolf each took a cigar, along with Vladimir, who pulled out of his pocket a flashy gold lighter and lit each one in succession. "Boys, generally speaking, I like adventure. And I've always wanted to find the lost continent of Atlantis."

"That's just a story, boss," Jeb replied, flicking his ashes into an antique ashtray on the side table nearby.

"Not so, Jeb, not so. I've done a lot of research, and I'm convinced it's a real place. Most people believe it's underwater near the Bahamas. You two ever been to the Bahamas?"

"Yeah," Wolf said. "I like it there. Rum, gambling—what's not to like?" Vladimir and Jeb laughed.

"Exactly," Vladimir replied. "'What's not to like?' Anyway, I am putting together a team of explorers and researchers and securing a large sea vessel that'll be able to hold fifty or so people and carry diving equipment and drilling apparatus. We're leaving in February. I want to know if you'd like to be a part of the team." Vladimir took a long drag on his cigar and looked at Jeb.

"Well, we're not divers, boss," Jeb replied. "What do you want us to do?"

"Just be on hand in case I need you," Vladimir replied cryptically. "I'll pay you well, and if there's something special I need you to do, we'll talk about further compensation. I think we'll be gone until June, unless we get lucky before that. How does that sound?"

Jeb and Wolf looked at each other and grinned. "Guess we could handle a trip to the Bahamas," Jeb replied. "Long as we get time off to go gambling."

"Of course!" Vladimir replied. "We'll be both on the boat and on Bimini, and we'll make available to you a small boat you can take anytime. Grand Bahama Island has some super casinos."

Jeb stood up. "Pleasure doing business with you, Vladimir. We're in."

The men shook hands. "Let's drink to it. Have some brandy, boys!"

Back at the reception, Essie, Rob, and everyone at the event had just finished eating. The carob cake was a knockout, and people were beginning to get a bit tired. The reception was beginning to wind down. "Jeremy?" Essie asked, "Can you get me my clutch? It's got my powder in it. It's in the coat room, at the end of the hall."

"Sure, Aunt Essie," Jeremy replied.

"Want some company?" Addison asked. "I need to stretch my legs, anyway."

"Okay, sure," Jeremy said.

The brothers got up from the table and headed out the main ballroom door and down the hall to the coat room. As they got closer, they saw a door open at the end of the hall. There were Vladimir, Jeb, and Wolf, shaking hands. Vladimir went back into his study and closed the door behind him. Jeb and Wolf began walking down the hall and, seeing Jeremy and Addison, stopped in their tracks. "Well, if it isn't Vladimir's henchmen," Jeremy said, loud enough for Jeb and Wolf to hear.

"I believe you're right, Jeremy," Addison said. "Hey, Wolf, your face looks a lot less swollen since the last time I saw you," he added.

"No thanks to you, cyborg," Wolf replied, walking toward them, with Jeb right behind. "I ought a take you outside right now and teach you something."

"You've got nothing to teach me," Addison replied, laughing. "But I could teach you right out of this life!"

"That's enough of that," Jeb said, getting in between the two. "Hey, we're all friends now. Didn't you get the memo?"

"No, we didn't," Jeremy replied. "We're no friends of yours."

"Well, the boss says we are," Jeb responded. "He said to us, he said, 'All's well that ends well.' Come on, Wolf; let's go." Jeb led his friend out past Addison and Jeremy, to their car, and the two thugs sped off.

Back at the reception, Aunt Essie and Rob had changed their clothes. Then Aunt Essie threw her bouquet to a group of laughing women, each of whom was hoping to catch it. Rob and Aunt Essie descended the stairs and waved good-bye to everyone at the reception. They headed out to a waiting limo that had at its rear the requisite cans on strings and a Just Married sign.

As Rob and Essie left the reception on their way to the airport, Jeremy and Addison wondered what another connection between Vladimir and the thugs might portend for them. "I don't know what that was all about," Jeremy said, "but I don't trust those two. It can't be good."

Addison sighed. "Yes," he said. "I have to agree with you. I'm not convinced about that whole 'all's well that ends well' thing. I think, my dear brother, that we will just have to see what happens!"

ABOUT THE AUTHOR

J eremy Q. Taylor & The Cyborg In The Cellar is a fun, suspenseful sci-fi book that takes the reader on an adventure in the not-too-distant future involving a perfect cyborg and a none-too-perfect teen boy.

A tale aimed at "tweens"—those youth ages 9-12—but equally enjoyable for all, the book explores questions of good vs. evil, spirituality, and more. These themes are cleverly woven into a fast-moving plot involving an idealistic scientist struggling as a single parent, typical American teenagers, and a greedy businessman with his own plans for that cyborg.

Growing up with two rambunctious siblings in New York, S. Pepper always had a book in her hands, and was often told by teachers that she should write for a living. An MBA led to a fulfilling career in education products marketing, and now Ms. Pepper is finally pursuing her dream of writing books for pre-teens.

"I have always had a passion for the future and our spirituality," says Ms. Pepper. A big fan of The Terminator movie series, she wants pre-teens to ask themselves, "What does it mean to be human? Are we simply our DNA or are we more? How soon might cyborgs be living among us?"

She feels that middle schoolers are the perfect audience for her questions, because of their open attitudes and self-discovery at this age.

S. Pepper currently lives in Morgan Hill, CA, with her husband and daughter.

CPSIA information can be obtained at www.ICGtesting.com
Printed in the USA
LVOW08s0111291013

358966LV00001B/75/P